in the psychic's wagon . . .

"You're getting tired," Tara said, her voice almost melodic.

Tess couldn't help it, she shut her eyes.

"You feel as if you want to sleep," said Tara. "You're even tireder still," and the soothing tone of her voice caused Tess to almost drift into sleep.

She'd never felt like this before with her eyes closed. She was starting to see imagery—yes, her eyes were shut—she couldn't quite explain, like a field of blue that flipped to green, so bright, almost like an image on a TV screen. She felt like she was floating. She had this strange sense that she was actually floating up against a blue/green screen.

Tara whispered to her, "Touch the sky," and that was the last thing Tess remembered . . .

. . .

OTHER BOOKS YOU MAY ENJOY

CARNIVAL MAGIC

AMY EPHRON

PUFFIN BOOKS

PUFFIN BOOKS
An imprint of Penguin Random House LLC, New York

First published in the United States of America by Philomel Books,
an imprint of Penguin Random House LLC, 2018
Published by Puffin Books, an imprint of Penguin Random House LLC, 2019

THE LIBRARY OF CONGRESS HAS CATALOGED THE PHILOMEL BOOKS EDITION AS FOLLOWS:
Names: Ephron, Amy, author.
Title: Carnival magic / Amy Ephron.
Description: New York, NY : Philomel Books, [2018] | Companion to: Castle in
the mist. | Summary: While visiting Aunt Evie in Devon-by-the-Sea, England, Tess
and Max are whisked away by a magical carnival in need of rescue. | Identifiers: LCCN
2017050515 | ISBN 9781524740214 (hardback) | ISBN 9781524740221 (e-book) |
Subjects: | CYAC: Carnivals—Fiction. | Wishes—Fiction. | Magic—Fiction. | Brothers and
sisters—Fiction. | England—Fiction. | BISAC: JUVENILE FICTION / Fantasy & Magic. |
JUVENILE FICTION / Family / Siblings. | JUVENILE FICTION /
Social Issues / Friendship.
Classification: LCC PZ7.1.E62 Caq 2018 | DDC [Fic]—dc23
LC record available at https://lccn.loc.gov/2017050515

Puffin Books ISBN 9781524740238

Printed in the United States of America.

1 3 5 7 9 10 8 6 4 2

Edited by Jill Santopolo.   Design by Jennifer Chung.
Text set in 12.25-point Winchester New ITC Std.

For Maia, Anna & Ethan,

whose love and imagination inspire me every day

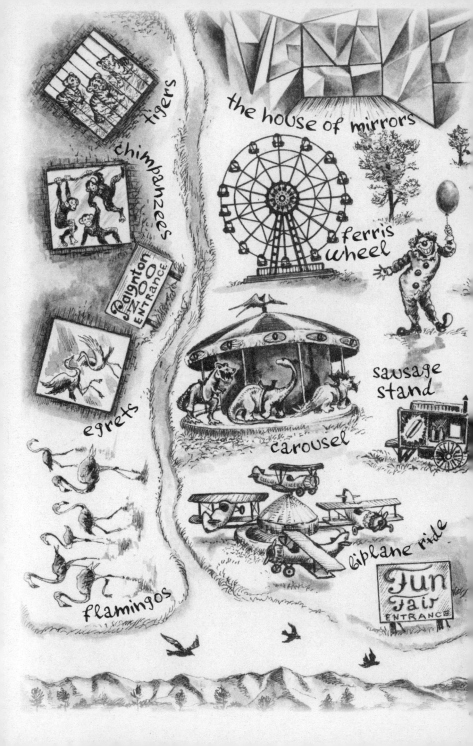

aunt evie's cottage

aerial ballet tent

farmstand

psychic wagon

traveller's wagon

CONTENTS

the cottage at devon-by-the-sea

I'll take the attic," said Tess, tearing up the third flight of stairs before Max even had a chance to fully understand the question.

"It's a three-bedroom house," Aunt Evie had said when they walked in the door, "four, if you count the attic. So, since your parents are coming in a few days, one of us has to take the attic... and I don't think it's going to be me."

"It's mine," said Tess emphatically. She thought an

attic bedroom was possibly a charming idea, a little scary but in a good way. It also occurred to her that her brother, Max, might be a little scared if he slept up there—even though he wouldn't want to admit it—so she instantly claimed it.

Tess hesitated on the landing at the top of the stairs. She held her breath as she popped the door open, frightened it might be dusty, musty, or dotted with spiders, but the room was flooded with sunlight from a triangular window that looked out on to the sea. It was a small room—well, tiny, but blue-and-white striped wallpaper lined two of the walls, and the wall with the window was painted white so that it was almost cheerful.

There was a double bed covered with a down quilt and big white pillows. The ceiling sloped down a bit like a triangle toward the window, so she figured she had to be careful getting out of bed on the right side.

Note to self: remember to always get up on the left side of the bed so as not to bump your head.

Tess could hear the sound of the ocean lapping softly against the shore. And even inside the air was fresh, a tiny bit salty and moist from the sea. It occurred to Tess that she was really going to like Devon-by-the-Sea on top of that strange thing that had already happened that she didn't think she could tell Aunt Evie about.

a plane, a train, a car ride, and a trip to the zoo

here's what had already happened

Their mom, Abby, had taken them to the international terminal at JFK Airport. They checked in with the help of a very nice porter who told them, after he helped carry their bags to the counter, that he hoped they had an excellent adventure.

Tess hoped they had an excellent adventure, too.

Their mother then escorted them as far as she could, to the security line.

Tess dropped her backpack. She hugged her mother and gave her a kiss on both cheeks since, after all, they were going to Europe, and kissing people on both cheeks was the custom there. Max just nodded when his mom smooshed his hair on the top of his head, which was a funny way she had sometimes of sending him off to school in the morning. But then he dropped his backpack, too, and gave her a hug and a kiss on the cheek. Then Tess and Max were on their own.

They waited patiently in line for their turn to go through the metal detector. Max went first. Then Tess.

For reasons Tess couldn't understand, when she walked through the metal detector, there was suddenly a very large noise as the alarm went off. She turned around. She was certain she couldn't have done that. But everyone at the checkpoint was looking at her. The TSA officer, who wasn't nearly as nice as the porter, directed her, as if it was a command, to walk back through the machine.

"It must be my cap," said Tess instantly, realizing she'd forgotten to take her olive-green baseball cap off. It didn't have any lettering on it at all, no advertising; it didn't draw any attention to itself, just kept the sun off, which is what Tess thought was the perfect thing for a cap. She gently placed it on the conveyer belt.

"Are *you* wearing a belt?" the TSA officer asked her.

"Nope." She shook her head. Then wondered if *nope* was the right thing to say to a TSA officer.

"Is your cell phone in your pocket?"

"No," she answered.

"Do you have any keys?" he asked her.

"Oh," she said. *She was frightened he was going to take it away from her.*

She pulled an old-fashioned skeleton key out of her front jeans pocket. "Of course! It's—the key to my aunt's house in London," she said.

This was the first lie Tess had told in a long time, but she knew she couldn't tell him what it was really. *She was frightened he might ask to see it.* It was the key to the gate at the castle next door to her aunt's house in Hampshire, the key to her friend William's garden, but that seemed way too hard to explain . . .

When Tess was packing, she'd heard William's voice so clearly, as clearly as if he was standing next to her, saying the last thing he'd said to her last summer. "Keep the key," he'd said, "you never know when you might need it."

Tess thought it was opportune of her to take the skeleton key with her to England—that was a word their Dad used, "opportune," it implied it might be useful later—and

Tess thought that might actually be the case because, in her experience, you never knew what could happen in England.

"We need it," she said to the TSA officer, her voice pitching up a little bit when she said it.

Her brother, Max, chimed in from the other side of the checkpoint, "We do. Aunt Evie said we should bring it." Max was lying, too.

The TSA officer hesitated for a moment. It felt like a long moment to Tess. "All right, then," he said, finally, without asking to see it.

She'd been so frightened he would ask to see it. She never was quite sure what the key was going to do if she handed it to someone else. She remembered what had happened when Max had found it by mistake last summer and it had turned bright red and burned his hand . . .

"Is this your backpack?" he asked. The TSA officer pointed to a kid-size version of a military-green backpack sitting alone at the end of the conveyor belt that in fact belonged to Tess. "Do you think you could put that key in your luggage, where it belongs?"

"Yes, Sir," she said. He handed it back, around the X-ray machine, and watched while she unzipped the side pocket, carefully dropped the key in, and zipped the pocket back up. She realized she'd been holding her breath. She had been so frightened that he might confiscate it, another one of those grown-up words that meant "take it away." She set the backpack on the conveyer belt and watched it slide again into the metal tunnel, where a picture could be viewed. Then she stepped back through the metal detector, and thankfully neither she or the backpack set off any further alarms.

Almost the second the plane leveled out at flying altitude, Max fell asleep.

Tess wrote a story in her notebook about a little girl who falls asleep on a train and misses her stop, rides past it, and ends up in another town—that was as far as she got and then she fell asleep, too.

Tess and Max woke up almost at the same moment, somewhere over the Atlantic.

Their mom's best friend, Franny, had packed them sandwiches from the fancy delicatessen so that they wouldn't have to eat the food on the plane, which she said was full of preservatives. Their mom had slipped in some chocolate chip cookies after Franny left. They were from the bakery on the corner but they weren't sure Franny believed in sugar, either.

Tess and Max were both surprised how quickly the

pilot announced that they were about to land at Heathrow Airport.

They put their seatbacks up and Max raised the window shade, which was especially startling as the sun was just beginning to rise. The clouds were stunningly tinged with gold, blue, red, and purple rays, like a painting, and the outline of London looked like a toy city with its pitched roofs, cobblestone streets, and church steeples covered in a cloud of mist.

• • •

Aunt Evie was waiting for them at the airport. Tess heard her voice before she saw her.

"Yoo-hoo," her voice rang out clearly through the crowd.

Aunt Evie had lightened her hair. She also had a new haircut. The front was layered a bit and fell beautifully around her face and down her shoulders, and she was wearing a bit of makeup and what looked to Tess like a *new* summer dress. Tess didn't know if her aunt was feeling "chipper," an English word for "cheerful," or if it was just the way Aunt Evie dressed to go to London, but either way Tess thought her mom would think it was a good sign:

that maybe Aunt Evie was cheering up, coming out of her shell a bit. Aunt Evie had understandably been sad since her husband, their uncle John, had died so unexpectedly in a skiing accident three winters before. She had moved to their country house in Hampshire and practically holed herself up alone for a year and a half except for the month last summer when Tess and Max visited her. Aunt Evie was only thirty-nine, which their mom said was very young to be a widow. Aunt Evie was wearing a yellow sleeveless summer dress and high-heeled sandals.

Max made her smile when he said instantly, "You look awfully pretty, Aunt Evie." It was the first they'd seen her in almost a year.

Tess and Max had spent the school year in New York City with their mom. Their dad, Martin Barnes, a well-known newscaster and sometimes war reporter, had left in February.

He'd been made the head of the news desk in Berlin, which didn't really mean he was in Berlin. Berlin was mostly used as a jumping-off spot to parts of Europe, Russia, and the Middle East, so they were never quite certain where he was and if they were supposed to be worried about him . . .

Their mom, Abby Barnes, had stayed in New York

with them so that they could finish out the school year, Max, fourth grade, and Tess, fifth. Also, their mom was a writer and she had a book due.

Their mom and dad hadn't seen each other for three months, so they were going on a grown-up mini vacation, a long weekend, to Barcelona, Spain. Their mom's plane was leaving a few hours after theirs and the plan was, their mom and dad were going to join Tess, Max, and Aunt Evie in Devon-by-the-Sea. And maybe even take a trip to Scotland.

Aunt Evie had rented out her house in Hampshire for the summer and had rented a charming beach cottage in Devon, or as she called it, "Devon-by-the-Sea," which was really just a geographical designation, but when Evie said it, it sounded as if it was a magical name.

Aunt Evie had planned and researched everything in the neighborhood. There was wi-fi in the cottage and also a big, high-definition flat-screen TV on a wall in the living room. The cottage was "turn-key furnished," which means it came with practically everything: tables, chairs, couches, sheets, towels, pots, and pans.

There was a miniature golf course nearby, a cherry festival coming up, and a world-famous zoo that was also an animal refuge, not to mention the actual beach and the sea itself and lots of other children potentially around.

Aunt Evie really wanted Tess and Max to be happy and occupied this summer. She'd even bought an iPhone herself, so that they would always be able to reach her, and she'd set up an Instagram account, even though she wasn't exactly up-to-speed on how to post on it. Her Instagram handle was @YrAuntEvie. The first photo she posted was a view out the living room window of the beach cottage in Devon-by-the-Sea, the day she rented it. The wood window frame was almost like a frame to the view in the picture. The sky was gray, the ocean was a little gray, too, with tiny white tops to the waves, and white sand, like a washed-out watercolor.

She added a caption.

Guess where I am?

Answer: Devon-by-the-Sea

Max figured it out instantly, though the location was obvious because she said that right in the caption. "Do you think she's rented a beach house?" he asked his mom, showing her the picture. Her mother knew the answer as Aunt Evie had called her to discuss the plan. "Yes, Max," she answered, "I think she has. Although she called it a turn-key cottage."

Max asked Tess if she thought there were any ghosts in

the cottage. Their mom overheard and answered instantly, "I'm not sure that's what turn-key means." But Tess and Max, who'd been on a trip to England before and had a very curious experience with a key, weren't sure that they agreed.

• • •

From Heathrow, they took a taxi to Paddington Station in London. In the back of the cab, Tess unzipped her backpack and put the skeleton key safely in her back pocket.

They boarded a train to Exeter, approximate train travel time three and a half hours, according to Max, who looked it up on his iPhone. They arrived three minutes early.

Aunt Evie had parked her blue Bentley at the train station earlier that day. It was comforting to see it there (and a little bit exciting), like running into an old friend. Tess sat in the back seat, as usual, so Max could sit in the front seat as he sometimes got carsick. Aunt Evie put the top down and tied her hair up in a ponytail.

Tess looked out the window as they drove. The landscape was so green, what their mom would call "pastoral," high grass dotted with wildflowers. They headed south on the windy highway, which curved left, then right along the countryside. Tess saw a young woman with long brown hair tied back loosely under a riding cap, riding on a spectacularly beautiful chestnut-colored horse, pedigree, for sure. The woman was wearing a fancy jacket and breeches, English riding pants, and boots that looked like they could walk on their own. But what struck Tess most was the single fluidity with which she rode, as if she really was one with the horse.

Tess had a sudden idea. She thought it would be amazing to ride a horse on the beach at night. She was careful not to wish for it. She knew from last summer that it was best to save your wishes for things that might be *really* important. But she thought she might tell her aunt about it later, just in case there might be a stable in the neighborhood where you could rent a horse for an afternoon or an evening.

The woman riding looked over at Tess for a moment and nodded and then seemed to race along with them, keeping pace with the Bentley, until a wide open field came into view and the woman guided the horse to make a right turn and then raced away, leaving a trail of brown dust in their wake before they seemed to disappear.

• • •

Aunt Evie drove for a while down the highway, then unexpectedly made a peculiar turn, almost a U-turn but not quite, a turn around a roundabout and then a right turn into a driveway and past a sign on a building on the left that said Paignton ZOO. The word *ZOO* was in capital letters. "I thought we'd stop and get tickets," she said, "so we can go here another day."

Max tried to explain to Aunt Evie that you probably didn't need to buy tickets in advance, that it wasn't like a concert or the theater.

"Yes, I know that," said Aunt Evie. "I just thought, we'd have to wait in line the day we *went* to the zoo, and what would be the fun of that when you could already be animal-watching?"

Sometimes it was hard to argue with Aunt Evie's logic. They obediently hopped out of the car the moment she parked and followed her to the ticket line. There was a line. She was right about that.

Tess said to Max, "Stay with Aunt Evie. I want to take a little walk around. Is that okay, Aunt Evie?" Tess's legs were tired, cramped, from so much travelling—the plane, the taxi, the train, and the car—and she thought it might do her some good to stretch her legs *and* take a tiny peek at the zoo . . .

Tess walked down the paved walkway toward the entrance and made a left turn to where an Indian gentleman, wearing a gray-and-white pin-striped suit, who spoke in a very proper English accent, was guarding the entrance. "Do you have a ticket, Miss?" he asked, when he saw her lingering by the turnstile.

"No," said Tess, "not yet. My aunt's waiting to buy advance tickets." She gestured to Max and Aunt Evie standing in the line at the ticket booth. "Tickets for another day," Tess added just to be clear.

"I guess your aunt"—he said it the British way, the way Evie insisted, *awnt* instead of *aunt*—"believes in pre-planning. I could let you go in for a peek, if you want," he said. "But you have to be back in six and a half minutes. Exactly six and a half minutes."

The gatekeeper did look like someone who would be incredibly precise.

"Got it," said Tess, checking her iPhone for the time. "Thank you." She gave him a thumbs-up and a smile. He gave her a thumbs-up back.

Tess practically ran through the glass doors. She wanted to see the giraffes. Tess's mother had told her once that she thought giraffes were an animal with perfect posture! Tess smiled when she remembered that. Tess wondered if giraffes ever danced and if they did, what that would look like.

She hurried past the flamingos and the somewhat other-worldly aviary enclosed with netting and glass, filled with tropical trees and flowers, and a funny mist, and an extraordinary assortment of birds. Two egrets were apparently having a fight in the air, but she didn't stay to watch that.

She walked a little farther and watched a pair of chimpanzees swinging on a version of a jungle gym, mostly constructed from branches. The chimpanzees were grunting and making funny noises, panting—hooting as if they were deep-voiced owls—seemingly speaking to each other. The bigger of the chimpanzees hung by one arm. He turned and stared at Tess, as if he was trying to stare her down, and seemed to break into a chimpanzee laugh. Tess laughed, too. They were really funny. He got bored with staring and swung off to meet his sibling. She assumed they were siblings; their coats were the same color and they had such an easy familiarity with each other.

Tess heard a faint sound up ahead. It sounded as if there was a little kid in distress, whimpering, as if he (or she) were lost or hurt. She hurried down the walkway.

Tess turned and, in a cage to the left of her, saw three

baby tigers lying on a bed of straw. Two of them were perfectly content, it looked like. The third one, the tiniest of the three, was writhing on the straw, as if he or she (Tess couldn't tell if it was a girl or boy tiger) was in pain. The baby tigers were so beautiful, their coats soft and shiny, their stripes not quite formed so that it looked as if there were spots of black against their pale, golden fur, dark, bright eyes, almost sparkly, the tiniest wisp of whiskers, and their pink tongues, like the most beautiful baby cats. The smallest one was definitely in some kind of pain.

Tess looked to see if there was a zookeeper or anyone vaguely official-looking around, but all she saw were other visitors to the zoo. The baby tiger looked up at her sadly and cried again, this time distinctly, so there could no mistaking that it was a cry for help.

Tess couldn't stop herself from trying to help.

She kept very still and approached them very quietly. She thought that was a good idea. She sat down cross-legged in front of the chain-link fence, barely taking a breath, so as not to alarm any of the baby tigers. And then, very slowly, she reached her hand out, palm turned upward, almost the way a tiger would expose its paw.

The baby tiger followed her and held out its paw, too, and turned it over, almost as if it was imitating Tess. Not really. Almost as if she wanted Tess to look at it. Tess was sure it was a girl tiger now, although she couldn't have explained exactly why she thought that. The tiger continued to hold her paw out, as if it *was* the paw that was the problem . . .

Tess took a deep breath—Tess knew that what she was about to do was dangerous—a baby tiger wasn't like a baby kitten, and technically there were three of them.

Tess reached her left hand through the bars and into the tiger cage, steadily and slowly, so slowly, until her fingers were lightly touching the toes of the tiger's right paw and the tiger's toes were touching Tess's fingertips. Tess dropped her hand below the tiger's paw and gently held it up. She leaned in and looked closely, examining it, studying it, turning it to the side and back again, at no small risk to herself as the baby tiger's nails shot out as if it might be about to scratch her.

"Shssh," Tess said softly and surprisingly calmly, "I'm not going to hurt you." She turned the paw back again and saw something reflecting from it.

There was definitely something shiny sticking up between the second and third toe, something that Tess thought shouldn't be there at all. She didn't think tigers were supposed to have metal-looking things in their paws.

She wondered for a moment if it was a tag or something, a kind of tracker or identifying mark that had been put there by a zookeeper, but if it was, it wasn't put in to the proper place or in the proper way because Tess could see it must hurt every time the baby tiger walked. It might hurt even when the tiger cub wasn't walking. It looked as if it was very sharp.

Tess instinctually reached into her back pocket for the skeleton key. She wasn't sure why she did that. But sometimes the key was illuminating. She held it in her right hand and moved it close, like it was a flashlight or something. And then the key seemed to have a power of its own, as it almost magnetically drew itself to the tiny piece of metal and Tess heard a click as they connected.

She whispered to the baby tiger, "This might hurt a little bit."

She pulled the key back gently, stopped for a moment, held her breath, and then with rapid precision and amazing aim, she pulled out of the baby tiger's paw what turned out be to a silver needle seemingly magnetically affixed to the key.

She pulled the needle off the key and quickly deposited the key back into her jeans pocket, hoping that nobody had noticed. She then looked closely at the needle in the palm of her hand. She was quite certain it was a needle as the top end was slightly larger than the sharp, pointed bottom and seemed to have an eye. She thought it was silver. Steel? It was very strong for a slip of metal, tiny as it was, almost unbendable, and the point was razor-sharp.

As Tess held it up, it seemed to give off sparkles, bright sparkles, yellow, silver, gold, blue tinged with orange, and back to gold, as if it was reflecting in the sun. The light it gave off was so bright, it occurred to her it might have a power of its own. *There she was, imagining things again.* She closed her hand around the needle tightly, being careful not to poke herself, as it was awfully sharp.

She held the needle up again and it seemed to embrace the sun, reflect it, so that she and the tiger were bathed in a halo of light. The chain-link fence was no longer visible. It was as if she was sitting on a wild field of grass with the baby tiger and all around them were trees, flowers, and the sway of a tropical breeze. The tiger seemed to stand slightly above her on a hill as if they were or had been for a moment transported to India, the sound of an elephant in the distance and some kind of exotic music. *She must be imagining it.* She put the needle down and it was as if the image disappeared, the chain-link fence was back, and Tess was sitting still in front of the tiger's cage. Tess quickly slipped the needle into the right front pocket of her jeans.

Of course she'd imagined it, and why wouldn't she have heard an elephant in the distance? After all, she was at the zoo.

But Tess could still feel the vibration of the exotic music, hanging in the air like a tropical heat wave infused by the scent of exotic flowers, the rhythmic pounding of some kind of string instrument accompanied by a drum. Yet, there was no music playing, just the sounds of "Oohs" and "Ahhs" and sighs of relief as Tess realized a small crowd had gathered and had been silently, as if they'd all been holding their breath, too, watching her interaction with the baby tiger. She could hear some of them whispering now. One little boy saying to his mother, "Did you see what she did?"

Tess heard a noise in front of her in the cage as the mother, or was it the father, tiger appeared right next to the bars and opened the jaws of his or her mouth and roared so loudly that the sound almost seemed to shake the cage. Tess stepped, well, actually she jumped back, frightened, and then looked at the tiger and realized it might be a triumphant roar, sort of a thank you and a celebration, if there was such a thing. She figured she'd better not stick around to find out. Tess started running quickly—not as if she was running away but running back, as she'd promised the man at the entrance that she would be back in six and a half minutes and she was worried that she might be late.

As she ran back through the open glass doors, the elegant Indian gentleman, the gatekeeper, or zookeeper, or whoever he was, shook his head and gave her a curious smile.

"You're lucky you didn't get hurt in there," he said.

Tess wondered if there were cameras inside the zoo and he had a monitor, some way he could see what was happening inside the zoo. *That would make sense, wouldn't it? That could be a logical explanation.* But there weren't any cameras visible and no screens. And, well, it was curious, because it was almost as if he knew what she'd done . . .

"Thank you," said Tess as she passed him.

"No, Miss," he said, bowing slightly when he said it, "I think I'm the one who should be thanking you."

Aunt Evie and Max were waiting at the car. Tess slid into the back seat and fastened her seat belt. "The gate-keeper let me into the zoo for a minute," she said.

"And?" asked Aunt Evie.

"And . . ." said Tess. She hesitated. "They have an

aviary, giraffes, but I didn't get to see them, and I don't know what else, three adorable baby tigers. They're really adorable," she said.

She decided not to tell about exactly what had happened. It was sort of hard to explain. They might think that she was imagining things again. Or else Aunt Evie might think she had unnecessarily put herself in danger. Her dad said sometimes she didn't think long enough before acting, that she just operated on instinct, which was a good and a bad thing. "They're very adorable," said Tess again.

"Apparently there's a crocodile swamp and pythons," said Max, who was reading a pamphlet.

Tess wasn't sure how she felt about that, but Max was pretty excited. "I'm very glad we're going back," said Max.

Evie held up the envelope with the tickets in it as proof. "Any time we want," she said.

As Evie drove down the winding road, the sun was just beginning to set. Tess took the needle out of her pocket and held it up. It looked exactly like a needle, it had an eye, and it was the brightest color of silver. And, as the sun's rays reflected off it, it definitely seemed to give off sparks, yellow, gold, red, blue, almost like a halo around it. Tess shut her hand around the needle quickly and carefully slipped it back into the front pocket of her jeans.

She tried to think how she could explain it to Aunt Evie without making her nervous, but she didn't think she could explain it, at all.

waking up in devon

The next morning, Tess discovered that there weren't any curtains on the window in the attic bedroom. Nonetheless, she'd managed to sleep until half past ten. The light was streaming in, making criss-cross patterns on the white down quilt, not multicolored but black-and-white, as if the sun's rays had been filtered, washed out through the gray cloudy sky, and there were similar spots of light, black and white patches, on the hardwood floor. She snapped a picture with her iPhone. When she looked at it, it looked like a black-and-white photograph from the thirties. Tess checked. She hadn't added a filter to it by mistake, and the absence of color in the photograph was startling, as was the absence of color in the room. It was a little strange.

She made her bed. Both she and Max had taken baths the night before at Aunt Evie's insistence that they wash off all their dirt from travelling. Tess carefully hung her pajamas on a hook that was conveniently placed on the door, pulled on her navy-blue bathing suit, the straps of which crossed in the back and was ideal for swimming. Then she slipped on a pair of jeans and a blue-and-white striped T-shirt—what her mom would call perfect beachwear. By the time she was dressed, the sun was peeking out from behind a cloud, and the color seemed to have returned to the room. She could see the sea, small waves rolling in almost like clockwork. She wondered how cold the water was . . . She looked at the picture she'd taken again—it was still black-and-white. She must have hit a filter by mistake.

She ran downstairs to find Max and Aunt Evie sitting at the kitchen table. There was a basket of warm scones, fresh butter, and a jar of strawberry jam on the table. There was also a tiny jam jar filled with violets and peonies, a cheerful centerpiece, and a pitcher of orange juice, which Aunt Evie had squeezed fresh that morning. There were seven kinds of yogurt—seriously, seven, including coconut and pineapple—and a bowl of cut-up strawberries, blueberries, and raspberries in the refrigerator. The beach umbrella was folded up by the back door, propped up next to the folded beach chairs. There were beach towels and a beach blanket stuffed into an oversized beach bag that inexplicably said *Miami, Florida* on it in big orange letters. The bag also contained sunscreen, Aunt Evie's book, and gosh knows what else. Next to it were three boogie boards.

"I know. I thought we might go to the beach," said Aunt Evie, "but the sun hasn't quite come out today. It keeps disappearing behind the clouds. And, what is it, Max, a thirty-two percent possibility of rain?"

Tess resisted giving Max a dirty look. Did he really have to check the weather app?

"Your grandmother used to say," said Aunt Evie, "the first day of vacation is best used to get organized. So, how do you feel about doing some shopping?"

"Okay, Aunt Evie," said Tess politely, as she tried to hide her disappointment.

"And who knows," said Aunt Evie, with a mischievous grin, "who knows what we'll find by the side of the road."

shopping for summer

As they pulled onto the highway, there was the funniest wagon parked in a field. "Oh, the traveller's wagon," said Aunt Evie, pointing to the old-fashioned wagon, which had been perfectly restored and not modernized, as there was a very beautiful black Friesian horse idling in the field that was obviously its mode of transportation. "He comes here every year," Aunt Evie said, referring to the man sitting on a folding chair by the horse, playing a violin. "He never talks to anyone. He just parks by the side of the road and lives there. Your Uncle John and I used to have long conversations about who we thought he really was, whether he was just some eccentric person who liked to camp by the side of the road and this was where he summered. Uncle John said he'd heard that he was a musician, which sort of makes sense since he's often playing a violin. We stopped by one day to see if he had a hat out and was accepting donations, but he was very standoffish and seemed to be playing only for himself. Quite peculiar. But there's something reassuring about the fact that he comes here every year. I'm quite happy to see him," said Aunt Evie.

"Did you used to come here every summer, Aunt Evie?" asked Tess, as she'd never heard about Devon-by-the-Sea before.

"I used to," said Aunt Evie, "when I was first married to your Uncle John. We used to think it was good luck to see the traveller's wagon."

"Then I'll take it as good luck, too," said Tess, who always felt as if they needed it.

They took a left turn down a single lane that zigzagged up a hillside. An actual single lane so that if you did run into another car going the other way, one of you had to actually back out. Aunt Evie said it wasn't going to be her because she wasn't very good at driving backwards. The lane was curiously lined on both sides by years-old hedges.

"Don't say it," said Tess.

As Max said in a very scary voice, "Beware of the hawthorn trees."

"Stop it," said Tess. "That isn't even funny."

"What?" said Aunt Evie. "What are you two talking about?"

"Nothing," said Tess. "Max was just saying how pretty it is around here." She gave Max a dirty look, but he couldn't see it because she was in the back seat and he was staring straight ahead.

She made a *Note to self: don't walk alone on the hills at night even if you have a flashlight.*

Aunt Evie drove up another, slightly less windy road, stopping at a farm stand that sold fresh eggs, apple turnovers, cucumbers, summer squash, fancy lettuce, carrots, fresh herbs, dill and mint and rosemary, perfectly ripe peaches and plums, and something neither Tess or Max or Aunt Evie had heard of before called a tayberry. Or at least that was what the sign in front of the baskets of berries said.

"What's a tayberry?" Max asked the nice lady who was running the farm stand. The woman answered with a funny laugh. "A tayberry, y'ask? Would ya like to try one?"

"Well, I sort of wanted to know what it was," said Max tentatively, which made the farm stand lady laugh again.

"Oh, a cautious one," she said.

Aunt Evie dived in. "I would," she said. "They look like a tall raspberry, if a raspberry can be tall . . ."

The farm stand lady handed Aunt Evie two tayberries and Aunt Evie, who was game for almost any food experiment, instantly popped them into her mouth. "Oh, they're lovely," she said, "sort of a blackberry but a little more tart."

"That's exactly right," said the woman, "a cross between a blackberry and a raspberry. They're kind of new. A hybrid. From Scotland, named after the River Tay."

"Tayberries!" said Aunt Evie. "We'll take two baskets. I think it would be fun to make tayberry jam, especially since I have helpers," she said, looking at Tess and Max. "I wonder how much sugar you'd have to use in the jam. Tess?"

But Tess didn't answer. She was distracted by a white dove that had flown onto the branch of a white birch tree, curiously distinct and peacefully startling framed against the brown-edged peeling lines of bark on the tree. In New York, doves were generally gray or brown. Actually, they were more like pigeons. And this dove was distinctive, like a white flower or a dusting of fresh snow.

"For what?" asked Tess after Aunt Evie repeated the question. Aunt Evie shook her head. "Tayberry jam," she said, "which I'm hoping you and Max will make with me this week."

"That sounds fun," said Tess as she looked at the peculiar berries Aunt Evie was buying. Aunt Evie also bought four ears of corn, insisting it was always a good idea to have extras just in case somebody unexpected dropped in for dinner. She'd said things like this so often that Tess wondered if Aunt Evie was expecting someone. Evie added a small basket of mixed summer squash, two cucumbers, green beans, fresh eggs, apple turnovers, lettuce, and a bunch of carrots with the tops cut off. She also bought two lemons and a lovely bunch of fresh mint that she said would be excellent for iced tea.

As they were driving back down the coast, Tess noticed a lot of commotion ahead on the side of the road.

"Look, see, oh, my!" said Tess.

Sometimes when Tess got excited she spoke in

one-syllable words. "Can we stop?" she asked Aunt Evie. "It looks like a carnival has come to town!"

"Look, see, oh, my," said Aunt Evie back, teasing Tess gently, but hitting the brakes as she said it. Aunt Evie made one of her famous beeline left turns, in this case almost a U-turn, driving the Bentley into the dirt by the side of the road. "They call them fairs in England," said Aunt Evie, even though one of the stands going up had a sign that said: CARNIVAL GAMES. "Fun Fairs," said Aunt Evie. There were tents starting to go up as well as a few trailers that looked like circus wagons, a Ferris wheel almost in place, and what looked like a small roller coaster under construction.

The tracks of the roller coaster were constructed of red and blue and yellow rungs, sort of like a kids' train set but instead of train cars, there were old-fashioned biplanes, each painted a different color, with fixed wings and an old-fashioned propeller, which seated two people in each. Each biplane had a name emblazoned on its side, in painted white handwriting with a corresponding image.

The crimson-red plane was called *Red Rocket* and, yes, there was a picture of a rocket, just to the left of the lettering, shooting straight up!

The bright yellow one was *Saturn's Rings*, and there

was a picture right above the letters of a round sphere, Saturn, surrounded by rings, and seven moons dotting up to the side.

The silver plane was named *The Flying Lady* and, of course, there was a painted picture of a lady who, except that she was also wearing a helmet, looked a lot like Aunt Evie when she put her hair up, tied a scarf around her neck, and put the top down on the Bentley.

The black plane was called *Lost in Space*. It was illustrated with an elaborate smattering of stars, tons of them close together at times, and geometric symbols. Or was it just one symbol, not quite like a triangle, more like a hexagon or, no, a very vertical, almost square-like six-pointed star. Tess looked at Max questioningly.

"I'm not sure," said Max, peering at the geometrical illustration, "but I think it might be a symbol for a quark or an equation for a quark."

"What's a quark?" asked Tess, although she wasn't sure she wanted to know. She knew what an equation was.

"I'm not sure I know," said Max. "But it has something to do with physics and maybe outer space?"

Aunt Evie smiled. She loved listening to their conversations. She thought Max and Tess were pretty funny sometimes, even when they weren't trying to be. But someone connected to the carnival also had a sense of humor. "'Lost in Space'?" said Aunt Evie questioningly. "I'm not sure I'd want to name an airplane that."

"It *is* a symbol for an equation," a voice behind them said. He was soft-spoken and he had a British accent. "That star you're looking at."

All three of them turned to look at him. He looked a lot like the gentleman they'd seen earlier at the traveller's wagon playing the violin who Aunt Evie had told them came to Devon every year and parked his wagon by the side of the road. Tess was pretty certain it was him, as he was holding in his right hand the lead to the reins of a black Friesian horse who was also somewhat identical to the horse they'd seen at the traveller's wagon. It looked as if the gentleman and the horse had gone for a ride and they, too, had stopped to watch the Fun Fair set up.

"What kind of equation?" asked Max.

"The quark part was right," he said. "It's the equation that some people say, not everyone believes in this, but some people do," he said, "an equation that potentially proves the existence of the possibility of an alternate universe. You know, the idea that right below where we're standing, underneath us, so to speak, right here, there could be another world, sort of like this one but not really; or just on the other side of the hedge," he pointed to a row of hedges that lined the other side of the roadway that Tess hadn't noticed yet, "there could be an alternate universe, sort of like this one but not really, the inverse sometimes . . ."

Tess and Max looked at him quite curiously. They'd had some experience like this before, at their friend William's castle last summer, although for reasons they couldn't quite explain, they never spoke about it.

"A world that's sort of like ours but different," said Max. "Just below us. Or just on the other side of the hedge."

"Exactly," said the gentleman.

"Are you a professor?" Aunt Evie asked the gentleman.

"Not really. Musician, actually," he said. "But I'm interested in mathematics."

"Hmm," said Aunt Evie. "I'm not sure how I feel about the idea of an alternate universe."

Tess didn't comment. She knew how she felt. A little bit wary and rightly so.

She was already entranced by his horse. She couldn't help herself. She lovingly, tentatively at first, stroked the horse's nose.

"Her name's Coco," the gentleman said, "and she's awfully glad to meet you."

"I'm awfully glad to meet you, too, Coco," said Tess. She stroked Coco's nose again and Coco's eyes caught Tess's in a friendly stare. But before any of them could say anything more, the gentleman mounted Coco, nodded as if that was a proper way to say good-bye, gave Coco a quick, gentle kick in the sides, and rode off down the road, leaving Tess, Max, and Aunt Evie alone to watch the Fun Fair set up.

"He never quite said who he was," said Aunt Evie. "I mean, he didn't tell us his name."

"We didn't tell him ours," said Max.

"That's true," said Aunt Evie. "But it was the gentleman from the traveller's wagon who comes here every summer." She said this almost as if it was a question.

Tess and Max both nodded.

"Supposedly he never talks to anyone, so I guess we should be flattered. Hmm," said Aunt Evie as if that was going to be her chosen word for the day.

A giant, royal-blue-colored tent was going up and there were carnival workers, including what looked like a tattooed lady; a clown who, even though he was dressed in white overalls, had on a red rubber nose and a painted-on smile; and two kids, wearing white T-shirts, stained from the dirt, and denim cut-offs, a boy and girl, who looked so much alike they were probably related, and who also looked as if they were about Tess and Max's age. Each of them was holding a big metal stake upright into the dirt just at the edges of the parachute-like blue silk tent, as a very tall guy, with a pointy beard, wearing a sleeveless T-shirt that exposed serious arm muscles, screamed loudly in a foreign language and brandished a big hammer as he walked purposefully around the tent, hammering each stake forcefully into the ground, and the enormous blue tent started to take shape to house the upcoming attractions.

In the distance, they could hear the sound of what seemed like a merry-go-round but which had an unusually high-pitched tempo, as if you could dance hip-hop to it, and Tess was sure she heard the faint beginning sounds of a flute.

"Yes," said Aunt Evie, smiling, before Max or Tess could even *start* to ask the question, "we *can* go to the carnival tomorrow, if it's open . . ."

a perfect day to go to the carnival

Max was making a list of things to tell Aunt Evie to try to convince her to let them go to the carnival by themselves . . .

1. *We take the subway home from school by ourselves. (Well, with each other, but it's the same thing . . .)*
2. *Mom lets us go to the skate park alone.*
3. *I go to D'Agostino's, the market on the corner,*

all the time for Mom. Especially on Sunday
to get fresh bagels or if she forgets something,
even if it's nighttime.

   4. Tess goes to dance class by herself.

"We take the subway home from school by ourselves. Well, with each other, but it's the same thing . . ." He said this aloud to himself, as if he was testing it out.

It wasn't that he didn't want to go to the Fun Fair with Aunt Evie, it was just that he thought he might be a bit embarrassed. He might not want to ride the biplanes if Aunt Evie was standing on the sidelines watching him . . . or even worse, riding with him in the plane.

"Mom lets us go to the skate park alone," he tried that one out loud, too. But it sounded kind of whiny, spoiled, rude. He didn't want to hurt Aunt Evie's feelings. He wrote one more reason down on his list:

   5. Tess is very responsible and always makes sure
that we don't get into any trouble or do any-
thing the least bit dangerous . . .

Max wasn't sure he could say that last one with a straight face. The amount of trouble Tess got them into last summer was pretty ridiculous. Or, if he was being really honest, the amount of trouble he'd gotten them into . . .

But then Max realized he couldn't say any of these

things to Aunt Evie, not after all the effort and care she'd gone to, renting the house in Devon to begin with, and inviting them to stay with her! He really didn't want to hurt Aunt Evie's feelings.

Tess was already downstairs. She'd dressed carefully, deciding to wear her sneakers and a pair of socks because it was probably dusty at the carnival and for sure they'd be doing a lot of walking. But she threw her sandals into her canvas shoulder bag. She was wearing her jeans and a sleeveless T-shirt, but she folded a long-sleeved T-shirt into the bag, too, in case it got chilly later. The weather in England was sometimes unpredictable. And she had a navy-blue cap—her favorite one, like a baseball cap but without any lettering, for protection in case the sun's rays were too strong. She also thought caps were excellent for hiding your true expression. Sometimes Tess couldn't help it and she rolled or squinted her eyes if she thought someone did something peculiar or impolite. With the baseball cap pulled down over her forehead, it was more difficult to see her expression. She was good at being deadpan, however, when it was required, excellent at not letting anybody throw her, but she didn't always remember to try to mask her expression.

It was a very pretty day. The sky was clear, the sun was

shining, but Evie didn't put the top down on the Bentley. Tess thought that was peculiar, but she didn't question it. When they'd driven about a mile, Aunt Evie stopped at a roadside café with a big sign in front that said LATTES, ESPRESSOS, and CHAI TEA.

Aunt Evie got herself an iced latte with a double shot of espresso and bought three bottled waters, handing one to each Max and Tess, and saying, "Be sure to drink a little bit of water today. It's not good to be out in the sun without drinking water," which sounded so much like their mom that Tess felt both happy and sad at the same time.

They got back in the car and Aunt Evie turned her head to look at Tess, who was sitting in the back seat, and then turned to Max, who was sitting in the front seat and said, "Family conference."

Uh oh, thought Tess. When their mom or dad announced a "family conference" it was usually because someone had done something wrong . . . or something bad had happened.

Tess and Max exchanged a look.

"Did we do something wrong, Aunt Evie?" asked Max.

"Oh no dear!" she said instantly. "I was wondering," Aunt Evie hesitated. "I was wondering . . ." she said again, as if she didn't know quite how to phrase this. "There's an antique show down the road. Well, just in the next town really. And, well, I don't know if your parents would approve, but I was thinking—I mean, you do sometimes take the subway by yourself in New York City. I know you indulge me, but basically you think antique shows are boring, I mean, who can blame you?"

"I don't think they're boring, Aunt Evie," said Tess. "You never know what you might find."

Max, who sometimes wasn't good at hiding his expression, either, shot Tess a look that clearly indicated that he did not agree. But he kept silent.

"We have weeks together," said Aunt Evie. "We'll find another antique show. What would happen"—she hesitated, stretching out the question—"if I dropped you and Max"—she was looking at Tess now, who was a year older than Max—"at the carnival by yourselves for an hour while I ran to the antique show and met you like an hour later? We'll pick a place. A place that's very findable, where we will meet? Well, it's eleven now. One thirty?" Neither Tess or Max remarked on Aunt Evie's math, that one thirty was actually two and a half hours, not one hour later.

Aunt Evie started the engine and pulled back onto the highway.

And Max heard her say to him, "After all, Tess is very responsible and always makes sure that you never get into *any* trouble."

Max felt himself blush. And then he wondered if Aunt Evie was psychic . . .

She wasn't really psychic, not in this instance, anyway.

Aunt Evie had heard Max. She hadn't meant to be listening. She'd been walking down the hallway and heard Max talking in his room. And since she knew Tess was already downstairs eating breakfast, she was sort of curious whom he was talking to. And then she realized, after she heard Max repeat a sentence one or two times, "We take the subway home from school by ourselves," that he was talking to himself. Testing lines out . . . Seeing how they played . . .

Aunt Evie kept waiting for Max to broach the subject. She watched him butter his toast, take a drink of orange juice. But he was quiet all during breakfast and didn't say a word on the way to the carnival except remarking on the fact that it was such a pretty day and that he was happy he'd brought his sunglasses.

Aunt Evie understood why it might be fun for Max and Tess to have an hour or two on their own. That was one of the nice things about the summer in general and going to the country or the seaside—that you can just be kids and run around on your own.

And, her sister Abby let them take the subway home from school by themselves, as long as they promised to stay together, so what could be the problem?

She pulled into the dirt parking lot outside the fair, driving underneath a festive banner with all manner of colored crowns and pom-poms interspersed with capital letters that spelled out FUN FAIR and underneath it another sign that spelled out GAMES, RIDES, and ADVENTURES.

"Are you sure you don't want us to come with you to the antique show, Aunt Evie?" Tess asked.

"I'm sure, Tess."

"Are you sure you don't want to come to the Fun Fair with us?" asked Max.

"It's okay, Max," said Aunt Evie. "It'll probably be good for you and Tess to have a couple of hours on the rides alone. I'm coming, just not for as long as you are . . ."

Aunt Evie insisted on parking and walking them up to the gate. "You have to promise me," she said, "that you'll stay together. Oh, and look," she said, "that's so funny: a merry-go-round with dinosaurs. I mean, that would be the perfect place to meet, don't you think, and that brontosaurus is so big you can see it from everywhere.

"That's it, then," said Aunt Evie, handing them each a twenty-pound note, which equaled more than twenty dollars. "I know it seems like a lot, but what if you get hungry, sometimes popcorn even costs two pounds! Ridiculous, if you ask me. Popcorn." And then she said something so Aunt Evie and so old-fashioned that Tess and Max almost started laughing. "Try not to blow it on a game of chance. The stuffed animals are never worth it."

Tess linked pinkies with Max and held them up, a public version of a pinkie swear. "Thanks, Aunt Evie," said Tess. "We promise. The brontosaurus at one thirty."

at the top of the ferris wheel

Aunt Evie was right. Popcorn: £2.00. And it was a really tiny bag, but it was fresh, right out of a popping machine, and it had real butter. Max got the popcorn and a shaved strawberry ice. Tess got a cotton candy, the pink fluffy sweetness that came out of nowhere and always seemed like it was magically made, except in England they didn't call it cotton candy, they call it candyfloss, which the person she bought it from informed her about when she ordered cotton candy.

"You mean, candy*floss*," he said, pointing to the mass of pink fluffiness forming in the bin. He smiled at her when he said it. "Not meaning to correct you, Missy"— he called her *Missy*—"just wanting to make sure I give you the right thing. Ben," he said, telling her his name, even though she hadn't asked him for it.

"Candyfloss, then, Mr. Ben," said Tess. "Yes, please."

"Mr. Ben," he said. "I like that. Candyfloss it is." He was also the popcorn maker and Tess took note that smoking behind him was a grill on which were sausages and buns, which might be excellent later if they wanted an almost proper lunch.

Tess and Max stayed quite close to each other, not quite holding hands, even though there weren't *that* many people at the carnival yet. They wanted to make sure they didn't lose each other in the crowd or get distracted and not notice where the other person had wandered off to . . . They walked past a wagon with a sign that said SNAKE CHARMER on the door, with an elaborate drawing of a snake that had endless coils, and then another wagon with a sign that announced a tattooed lady.

The line for the Ferris wheel wasn't that long. The baskets for the riders looked like chariots, elaborately painted red, with gold curlicues gilded onto the metal edging. The Ferris wheel itself was very tall.

"Imagine," said Max, "what the view will be like from up there. I bet we'll be able to see the sea." It was so like Max to think of something like that. He had a way of looking on to the future, which Tess envied, as she tended sometimes to jump in and not worry about where she'd jumped until later. Or rather try to figure something out once they were in trouble rather than before.

Of course, Max was right, the view from the top was pretty fantastic. They could see all the way to the sea and out to the horizon. But the second time they reached the top, there was a big grating sound that seemed to rock the entire ride and the Ferris wheel came to an absolute stop. And there they were, inside a chariot, hanging up on the top with no idea if it was ever going to start again . . .

This is when Tess started to think forward.

She tried to imagine scaling down the middle of the elaborate chains, gears, and metal pipes that constructed the Ferris wheel. She might make it, but she didn't know if Max would.

There was a bit of a wind, well, more than a bit really, and the chariot started to rock from right to left.

She started to imagine firemen coming to their rescue,

red fire trucks pulling up with their sirens blaring and lad-
ders . . . But it occurred to her that there probably wasn't a
ladder anywhere that would be high enough to reach the
top . . .

Someone on the Ferris wheel started to scream, and
then what sounded like a parent tried to quiet them.

Max was very pale.

"They're not going to let fourteen kids and four adults
fall out of a Ferris wheel," said Tess, "trust me on that one."

Max was impressed she'd counted that. Tess had done
it on purpose. She thought if she used "Max logic" on
Max that he wouldn't be scared. But she was nervous he
was going to get motion sickness as the chariot was seriously swinging back and forth.

"Don't look down, Max," she said. "Just look at me.
And if that gets boring, look at the sea. Don't look down!
You told me that we'd have a magnificent view of the sea
from up here, and boy, were you right! Look at that. You
can even see sailing ships out there. Do you think there are
whales in South Devon?"

"I looked this up," said Max. Of course he had,
thought Tess. "And it's rare to see a humpback whale in
Devon. It usually means they're in distress. They're supposed to stay further out in the Atlantic. In distress," said

Max who couldn't help himself from adding this, "sort of like us."

"We're really not in distress," said Tess in an effort to calm Max down as he seemed to get paler by the minute. "I mean, the Ferris wheel is a pretty stable object. It's just stuck. It's not like we're on a roller coaster."

Max had to admit she had a point. Being stuck on a roller coaster could definitely be dicier. It occurred to him that if a roller coaster got stuck, a rider could just keep on going, fly out of your seat, so to speak, and . . . he was definitely reassured that they weren't on a roller coaster. It was sort of pretty, looking out at the ocean.

In the process of trying to calm Max down, Tess had made herself a little anxious.

She tried to imagine a helicopter flying overhead and an elaborate rescue operation where she and Max were gently lifted and secured to a long hanging rope or chain that was then . . . She couldn't quite figure out what would happen then, if they'd come in for a soft landing or be pulled into the helicopter, or dangled for a while from the rope and then softly dropped into the sea, where a second coast guard rescue team would save them . . . She wondered what they called them in England, if they were called the Coast Guard?

"Take a sip of water, Max," said Tess. She was glad they'd brought their water bottles on the ride with them. She took a sip of water herself. The sun was beating down intensely. Max's cheeks were turning red, sunburned. Max thought he looked silly in a baseball cap and refused to wear them in public. Tess thought about offering to loan him hers, but she knew that he'd say "no" to that.

There was a terrible scratching noise as if the gears of the Ferris wheel were grating together but locked somehow and unable to move. Another scratching, almost scraping noise. A metallic thud. *Uh oh.* Then someone screamed.

She heard a woman gasp in fear. And then a deep breath as if the woman was trying to mask her cry.

Tess looked over to her right. One of the chariot's doors had opened and a little boy was half hanging out of his seat.

That was where the scream was coming from.

Everyone on the Ferris wheel was looking at that chariot and Tess heard another woman across from them gasp when she saw the little boy barely holding on. The woman muttered, "Sorry," under her breath as she realized it wasn't very helpful of her to have gasped, either.

The door of the chariot shut for a moment and the little boy righted himself. But then the wind kicked up, a big gust almost out of nowhere, and the door swung wide open again. The little boy was half-terrified. And the wind seemed to be winning. The little boy was half out of the chariot again and really having trouble hanging on. His mother leaned over to catch him, but then she was in danger of falling, too, and had to right herself before she got a grasp on him.

The little boy wasn't that far away from her, Tess reasoned, just one chariot over. She weighed the options for a second and in the snap of an instant made up her mind. Tess said to Max, "Just promise me you won't look down. Close the door after I leave and when I'm on my way back, please open it."

As if Max would do anything else.

He nodded and knew better than to argue with her. If this was going to work, Tess needed to believe in herself.

The little boy tried to scream again but it was as if the scream was caught in his throat, or he was so afraid, his voice had been chilled into silence. "It's okay," said Tess. "Just hold on."

She gingerly opened her chariot's door. Max held it open for her, being careful to hold on himself to an inside bar.

Tess knew she could do this. The arms of the Ferris

wheel were quite wide really, almost big enough to walk on if they had been on the ground.

The problem was they weren't on the ground, they were approximately sixty-five feet above the ground, and Tess knew that she shouldn't look down either. Crawling would be the best way. She tried a flat-out crawl on her knees, but after only one step, or a half crawl, she realized she was in danger of flipping upside down and then what would she do? Hold on with her hands and hope that someone came to rescue her? Jump down to the next tier, next metal bar, but then she'd have to crawl up that, which was at a 90° angle?

No, the only possibility she saw was lying down, flat as a board, and then carefully inching, inching—one knee, one arm, and a deep push forward from her center, as if she was propelling herself with her own breath—inching her way across the bar. Lying down absolutely flat and scrunching, inch-by-inch, until she reached the second chariot. As quickly as she could.

It was as if she was in a bubble and all sound stopped. And the only thing she could see was the Ferris wheel bar below her and the chariot ahead. Absolute silence. She reached to her front pocket. Something was digging into her. It must have been the needle. She managed to pat her pocket very gently and adjust it and then place her hand quickly back on the metal bar. As she did this, the light seemed to brighten as if there was a spotlight on her, guiding her way. Then a sparkle, as if there were stars. She looked up. She was certain it was daytime, but there was a cluster of stars above her. Well, more than a cluster, really, more like a blanket of stars sparkling and guiding her way.

By the twelfth crunch she was almost to the boy. "It's okay," she called out to him. "Hold on. Keep your eyes on mine. Can you do that? I'll be right there."

That wasn't really true—she had about eight more moves to go and it wasn't that safe to do them quickly.

His mom called out, "His name's Colin."

"Hey Colin, I'm Tess," she said as she kept on scrunching. No time to lose. Straight and steady. Keeping her eyes directly on him, but glancing down just to the bar to make sure she was still totally in balance . . .

Four . . . three . . . two . . . one. She was almost at a place where she could reach him.

"Can you follow directions, Colin?" she asked him. "Can you promise me that?"

Colin nodded.

"Okay, we'll do a pinkie swear on that when we're back on the ground. Okay? Deal?"

Colin nodded again and took a deep breath. He was half out of the chariot, but holding onto an inside bar.

"It's okay," she said to him. "It's going to be a little tricky. Don't let go of the bar you're holding on to. Got it?"

He nodded and inhaled again. "But with your other hand you're going to take my hand but be really careful not to pull me. Got it? Don't pull me. Or we both could go tumbling the wrong way."

Max from his perch in the other chariot was very glad she'd said this. He'd thought this exact thing himself. He'd concentrated very hard to try to send her a psychic message, as he was scared Colin might pull her over and they'd both go tumbling down . . .

The chariot that Colin was in was a tiny bit below the bar that Tess was resting on, so she reached down to him.

Colin reached for her hand as Tess reached a little farther down for his, trying very hard not to look down, which was almost impossible. They both missed. As if their hands just flew around and missed each other in the air. Someone wasn't aiming right. Tess realized she had to swing her arm down very gently or *she* might throw herself off balance.

"Wait, Colin. Let me put my arm out first." Tess

wondered how long she *could* balance on her knees just holding on with one hand, but she pushed the thought away and held her hand out directly.

"Reach for me," directed Tess. "Reach for me like you're going to touch the sky. But try not to move anything else."

With extreme concentration for a six-year-old, as that was all Colin was, he reached his arm and hand up to hers and as their fingers touched, she felt the sky lighten, as if it was daylight after all. She held tightly to his hand. "Don't squeeze me back," she said. "Just let me do this. Now, I'm going to put my hand on your back." She was lying flat again, one knee up, deep breath in, so that she had more strength to push with. And in one forceful move, she pushed Colin back into the chariot and his mother's arms. Colin's mom's eyes filled with tears, tears of joy. His mother quietly mouthed the words *thank you* to Tess.

But they weren't done yet. A gust of wind kicked up again and the chariot door swung open and shut and open again. Tess angrily and forcefully pushed the door back. But the door slammed and flew wide open again on its own. Tess tried it one more time, a little more gently this time, and Colin's mom caught the door, and held it, and Colin remarkably efficiently and triumphantly resecured the lock, sliding the silver bar back in. For emphasis, his mom refastened his seat belt, which shut with a defiant snap. And then she refastened hers.

This was fine, except a crowd had gathered beneath them. Tess was trying to use all her concentration to stay level on the bar, now lying absolutely flat, holding on with both arms. She heard screaming from the ground. She looked down for a moment, forgetting the rule, the absolute rule: *Don't look down.* And the world around her began to spin.

She held tightly to the bar and shut her eyes. When she opened them the world had righted and she squinched back carefully, sort of the way a caterpillar would move across the ground, but as quickly as she could.

The moment she was in reach, Max swung the door open, and as if she was a trained gymnast, she hoisted herself back into the chariot without missing a beat. She swore she heard screaming again from the ground but this time she didn't look down.

Max caught the door and mercifully closed the latch. Tess carefully put her seat belt back on. And the two of them did a triumphant pinkie swear because they couldn't help it.

There was another terrible screech and Max wondered

what would happen if the Ferris wheel went into free fall, sort of spun around all by itself as if it had no gears at all. He had the sense not to mention this thought to Tess, who sometimes had an even bigger imagination than he had.

And then, just as he and Tess were actually getting worried, there was a sound of an engine starting, another grating noise, deep and severe—Tess almost thought she saw sparks—and the Ferris wheel began to turn again.

But only for a second. And then it stopped. After a minute, it turned again, but only for a second. And then it stopped again. Then it began to turn again.

When Tess looked down—she couldn't help it, she had to see what was going on—she realized, with some relief, that it was turning like that on purpose so that each chariot could pull in and stop on the landing pad, and the riders could get off.

She and Max were almost the last chariot down. Tess felt herself breathe deeply as someone opened the chariot door. She practically pushed Max out of the chariot in front of her and then got out herself. She had a strange triumphant feeling when she stepped out onto the landing, as if a spotlight was on her, which she didn't quite make up, as someone was snapping pictures of her with a flash on, even though it was daylight. She looked up to confirm that. There weren't any stars in the sky. And she wondered if she'd imagined that, that blanket of stars in the sky. Colin and his mom were waiting for them on the landing. His mom had tears streaming down her face. She hugged Tess as she thanked her. During the promised pinkie swear, Tess insisted on a promise from Colin to be more careful in the future, which was accompanied by another flash of lights. Tess realized a crowd *had* gathered, including Ben, the grill master/popcorn maker/candyfloss man, who said simply as she passed, "I'm very happy to see you again, Missy."

Tess had to admit, she was sort of happy to see him, too.

*almost back on
solid ground*

Max was dizzy. Tess found him a fresh lemonade, which was excellent for settling stomachs. She got herself a lemonade, too. She wouldn't say she was dizzy, but her heart was beating fairly quickly. She sat down with Max on a funny bench, well, not quite a bench, more like concrete stools shaped and painted like mushrooms.

The clown they'd seen the day before was wearing a full clown costume now and performing in the crowd. He pulled a bright red ball out from behind a baby's ear, quite startling the baby's older sister, who couldn't have been more than two herself. Then he pulled a yellow flower out from the two-year-old's ear and when he handed it to her, she started laughing and clapping her hands and dropped the flower and started crying, which was sort of complicated and funny to watch. Except it got worse, because then he pulled a red balloon out from behind her other ear and gave her the string and she stopped crying for a second but then let go and, well, Tess wanted to give him a talking-to about being a nice clown.

But then the clown did the strangest thing. He was wearing very big clown shoes, at least twice the size of a normal person's foot or so it seemed, and he started rocking back and forth on them and then **j u m p e d** almost sixteen feet into the air and caught the string and rescued the balloon.

The clown seemed to hang there for a minute, almost as though the balloon itself could carry his weight, but that didn't make any sense. And then he bounced down and ceremoniously bowed to the little girl. But that wasn't all. He completely surprised her when he magically fashioned it into a balloon animal. It looked like a red panther to Tess, with a little bit of striping from a black balloon that he pulled out from behind his own ear. And then he took the red-and-black panther and tied it to the little girl's wrist with a swath of pink ribbon (that also came out of nowhere) just to make sure that it wouldn't fly away!

Holding pinkies now, because the carnival was getting a little bit crowded, and they were definitely too old to hold hands, Tess and Max walked over to the big blue tent they'd watched go up the day before. There was an elaborate poster pinned to the side of the tent announcing THE BREATHTAKING BARANOVAS with an elaborate drawing of an aerial trapeze and one young girl flipping in space from a swinging bar to another swinging bar with a young boy and a girl hanging upside down from it, waiting to catch her. The caption said:

THE BREATHTAKING BARANOVAS

Amazing Aerial Ballet Show!!

Starts promptly at 2:00 p.m.

"I've always wanted to try it."

"Try what?' said Max.

"Aerial ballet. Trapeze!"

"Of course you have," said Max.

Max had long ago realized that he and his sister were quite different creatures.

"I bet Aunt Evie would like this show. Two o'clock. Should we buy tickets now?"

Tess and Max both started laughing.

They remembered Aunt Evie making them go to the zoo to pre-buy tickets. But then Tess also remembered the baby tiger. She reached into her pocket and felt the sharp cold metal of the silver needle that she still had in her jeans. It seemed to almost give her a tiny shock when she touched it, and she swore she saw a flash of light. She pulled her hand out quickly.

She realized she'd put the skeleton key in her new sweater drawer at the cottage and left it there. Tess made a *Note to self: remember to always take the key. You never know when you might need it.*

She couldn't help but wonder if the needle had a power of its own—every time she touched it, there were sparks or halos of light—but maybe she was imagining it.

She waited in line with Max to buy tickets for the aerial ballet show.

Max said he wanted to ride on the whirligig but Tess reminded him he'd just recently recovered from dizziness and maybe they should wait a half an hour.

"Do you want me to try to catch a goldfish? Or you could do it," said Max. "I bet they have one of those silly games where you throw a ping-pong ball into a goldfish bowl and if you land it in the bowl, you get a goldfish. I've always thought that was sort of unfair to the poor goldfish, just sitting in the bowl waiting to see if a ball hit it," said Max but Tess didn't answer him.

Her eye was caught by something else. Just ahead another trailer, it looked like a circus wagon with wheels, with stars painted on it and a moon. And there was a sign in the window with blinking lights that said:

PSYCHIC

THE FUTURE IS
YOURS TO BEHOLD

Visible in the window, prominently displayed, was a crystal ball, the facets of which seemed to give off every color of the rainbow, glowing, sparkling.

"It might be a trick, Tess," said Max, almost as if he could read his sister's mind, "it might be lit from inside."

"And then again, Max," said Tess, "it might not be."

She was already three stairs up and had her hand on

the doorknob to the trailer. Max had no choice but to follow her. After all, they'd promised Aunt Evie they'd stay together no matter what . . .

As Tess was about to turn the knob, the door opened from inside. There was a strikingly beautiful woman with long blonde hair and slate-blue eyes, not like any color eyes Tess had ever seen before, blue and gray at the same time. And her age seemed indeterminate. She was forty or maybe twenty or maybe older or something in between. There was something kind of strange and ageless about her. She looked like a model in a magazine, except that she was a bit old-fashioned. She was wearing a long white dress, somewhere between a '60s flower child's and a Greek goddess's. She had a round headband resting on the top of her head, like a wreath, with pale white flowers woven onto it. "I knew there was someone there," she said. "I could simply feel it. And here, there are two of you. Well, come in."

Tess wanted to say, *If you're such a psychic, what's my name, then?* but she resisted (wisely) the impulse to be attitudinal with a psychic. The truth is, the idea that the woman might be the real deal both fascinated Tess and frightened her.

Tess stepped in instantly and Max had no choice but to follow her.

The inside of the trailer was exotic. There were white silk curtains on the windows, extra long so that they sort of puddled onto the floor. There were geometric rugs, maybe Pakistani, as they looked a bit like the rugs their mom's friend Franny had in her apartment, which she said were from Pakistan. The geometric patterns were complicated, orange, brown, black, and if you stared at one of them long enough, the images start to reverse, take new shape, go from square to diamond, and back again almost like an optical illusion on the floor. There was the strong scent of vanilla candles (or maybe it was incense), multicolored silk pillows on the floor that were big enough for sitting, antique lamps that seemed to shed an amber glow, all topped off by a star-crested chandelier that hung from the ceiling, slightly dim and bright at the same time, almost as if it was magically lit.

In the middle of the trailer was an elaborately upholstered daybed, elegant blue-and-white striped fabric and cushions that were edged in silver that looked like the most comfortable place to lie down.

"I'm so happy to meet you," the psychic said. "My name"—she extended her hand to Tess—"is Tara. And I suppose," she said, answering Tess's unspoken question from a moment before, "you must be Tess. You wonder how I know that? Well, like I said, I knew that someone was there and I've been expecting you. And you"—she turned to Max—"must be Max."

Max had to admit he was.

He shyly took Tara's hand when she offered it to him.

"I've heard about the two of you," she said, which sort of gave Tess shivers, as she didn't know quite what that meant.

"Is there anything you want to ask me?" asked Tara.

There was, actually. Tess wanted to ask her if she'd ever see her friend William again. But she was too embarrassed to ask the question. She thought Max would think she had a crush on William, which wasn't really true. It was just that she wondered if they went back to visit Aunt Evie in Hampshire, if William would still be living at the castle. And if the key she had would let them in the garden gate. She wondered if William wondered about that, too. So, it wasn't really that she was embarrassed, she was more frightened if she asked the question that the answer might be no. And Tess knew enough about wishing and wanting things to be true, that she didn't want to ask the question.

"No, nothing I can think of," said Tess.

"Well, there must be a reason you're here. How do you feel about being hypnotized?" Tara asked Tess.

"I've always wanted to be hypnotized," said Tess.

Somehow this didn't surprise Max. Tess really did want all kinds of things that never would have occurred to him.

"But," Tess continued, "I've always been afraid that I'm too—what do you call it—too strong-willed for it to work. Also, you'd have to promise that you wouldn't insert a secret command. You know, one of those things you read about in a story where if I hear a certain word, I have to turn around and gosh only knows what . . ."

Max had seen a movie like that once, too. Where someone was hypnotized and sent back to America to be a spy. "I'll be here to watch, Tess, if you really want to do it . . ."

"How much is it?" asked Tess.

Tara stared at her. "Well, I charge 20 pounds for an astrological reading. And 15 for a look at the cards." She held up a deck that looked kind of magical. "But you're not asking me for anything like that. And seeing as there isn't a line out the door today, I think it's 'on the house.' Or as me mum would say"—she suddenly sounded very English—"I'll take a ride on this one."

If Tess and Max had known how big a ride they were in for, Tess might have decided not to lie down . . .

tess gets hypnotized

The daybed was elegant and luxurious, with bentwood legs, the bottoms of which were in the shape of poodles' paws. Tess lay down as instructed but before she rested her feet, it occurred to her she ought *not* to put her shoes on the sofa. She sat up, untied her sneakers, placed them on the floor beside the daybed, and lay back down again. She stretched her toes out—it was much more comfortable to lie down when you didn't have your shoes on.

The sofa was very soft. She couldn't tell if the upholstery was silk or satin. It was light turquoise, but elaborately showy, with fine white embroidery making stitched patterns in the shape of stars. The cushions were stuffed with the fluffiest down so that she practically sank into it and Tess felt almost like she was floating.

The ceiling was painted a slightly darker blue. As Tess stared at it, she imagined (or maybe actually saw) the beginning twinkling of stars. That made no sense at all since it was daytime and she was inside a wagon. Tess wondered if that was a trick.

Her mom had never let them go to a storefront psychic even though Tess had asked, as there was one a block and a half away from their apartment in Greenwich Village. Their mother didn't think much of street psychics, not that she totally dismissed the idea of psychic abilities, she just doubted there would be a real psychic on the corner of Broadway and 10th Street. "Highly unlikely," she'd said. Her mom had once taken her to a Romanian tea reader. There was a tea room on the second floor of a building on Second Avenue. Her mom told her that she liked the tea sandwiches there, that the cookies were delicious, and that the "tea reading" was just a bonus. She let Tess have a cup of black tea, even though it was late in the afternoon.

She sat silently as the tea reader, an ancient woman who had piercing brown eyes, almost the same color as the tea, turned Tess's cup upside down and turned it up again and showed Tess the pattern made by the residual tea leaves that clung to the inside of the cup like a painting. It almost looked like a woodprint to Tess. There was something that looked like a tree and maybe some blades of grass and a funny, skinny river-like thing that ran almost up to the top of the cup on one side. Tess also thought she saw five stick figures, like a little kid would draw, that looked almost as if they were holding hands.

"You are going to have an excellent adventure," the tea reader said.

Hmm. Funny she remembered that. That was almost the same the thing the porter had said to her when he'd helped them with their bags at JFK. *You're going to have an excellent adventure.* Tess wondered if that adventure was starting now.

Tara, the psychic, had pulled a chair up and was sitting next to her. Even the chair was well-upholstered, with blue-and-white fabric decorated with pink flowers. It had no arms and the back of the chair was whimsically heart-shaped. It was a very low chair and Tara's face was very close to Tess's as Tess was lying down. She realized Tara did have the most remarkable slate-blue eyes that seemed as if they might be all-seeing. As near as Tess could tell, Tara wasn't wearing any makeup at all but her face was doll-like, smooth, unlined, and practically glowing.

Tara spoke softly as she directed Tess. "You're going to shut your eyes."

Tess did as she was told.

"And you're not going to hear anything except my voice," said Tara.

That wasn't exactly true as Max was still traipsing around the trailer, walking back and forth, scuffing his feet on the floor, bumping into things.

In the front of the trailer, built into the wall, was something that totally fascinated him. It was an elaborate fixture of pipes, and a wheel, and something that looked like a pulley, and sticking up from the floor, a gear box, sort of like something you might find on a ship or a tractor (not that Max had ever been in a tractor but he imagined it might be there). He almost tripped over it, making even more noise when he stumbled. He realized Tara was glaring at him.

Max knew it probably wasn't a very good idea to get a psychic mad. Let alone have Tess be mad at him . . . He saw what seemed like a built-in chair right in front of the pipe fixture on the wall, next to the gears, and in front of them, a circular thing that looked *almost* like a steering wheel. And so, he sat down in the chair.

Max realized it was like a captain's chair or a pilot's, he wasn't sure which one. And his legs didn't quite touch the ground, which was a good thing as it might be a guarantee that he'd be able to be still and quiet. He was fascinated by the gears and pulleys in front of him. Not to mention the funny thing that looked like a steering wheel.

Tess's eyes were shut, and to Tess, Tara's voice sounded like it was coming through headphones, stereophonic, as if each syllable had a beat of its own.

"All you're going to hear is the sound of my voice."

Tess opened her eyes for a minute and looked at the ceiling of the trailer. It was a darker blue, now. It looked almost three-dimensional. There was a crescent moon and a festival of stars, not like a constellation or anything, more like it was just the Milky Way or another galaxy without the image of the Big Dipper or Orion or anything recognizable, just a cluster of bright stars, some brighter than others, some awfully small. A DayGlo painting? Paint with glitter in it? That was all she could imagine. There was also a likeness of Saturn with its rings and the instantly recognizable three largest moons lining it. It was strange. Tess hadn't seen that when they'd first come into the trailer. The ceiling had looked kind of normal. Maybe she just hadn't noticed. She let her eye trace the line of the ceiling and there, just at the edge, was a painting of a landscape, rolling hills, and a fine line that looked like a horizon at the bottom of the sky.

"You're getting tired," Tara said, her voice almost melodic.

Tess couldn't help it, she shut her eyes.

"You feel as if you want to sleep," said Tara. "You're even tireder still," and the soothing tone of her voice caused Tess to almost drift into sleep.

She'd never felt like this before with her eyes closed. She was starting to see imagery—yes, her eyes were shut— she couldn't quite explain, like a field of blue that flipped to green, so bright, almost like an image on a TV screen. She felt like she was floating. She had this strange sense that she was actually floating up against a blue/green screen.

Tara whispered to her, "Touch the sky," and that was the last thing Tess remembered . . .

strange navigation

Max wasn't paying much attention to Tess. He heard Tara's voice in the background. *"The only sound you'll hear is my voice."* He purposefully tried to tune Tara out as it occurred to him that he might get hypnotized, too.

Max was studying the various mechanisms and what he assumed were control devices, including the nautical-looking metal wheel affixed to the wall in front of him. And because he was Max and he did things like this, he started to play with them, very, very quietly, because he didn't want Tara to get mad at him for making noise.

Max tentatively put his hand on a lever that looked a little bit like an on-and-off switch and then decided *not* to play with that. He pulled the wire of a pulley and realized at the top there was a handle. He wondered what would happen if he pulled it all the way down. He put both hands on the steering wheel and pretended he was driving an ocean liner. He put his right hand back on the lever. He couldn't help it. He flipped it up. And heard the strangest sound, almost like an underground engine. He tried to push the lever back into the down position, but the lever didn't want to cooperate. He tried again. It was definitely stuck in the up position. He put his hands on the wheel, which looked like it might be spinning. Well, it was spinning! To the right and then the left. He tried to put his hands on it in an effort to right it, but it was turning too quickly for him to grab hold. *No, he was imagining it all.* The wheel wasn't turning. But the lever was in fact up. Or maybe he hadn't imagined it and the wheel had stopped turning. Then Max started to hear an even stranger sound, like grinding rocks, or wheels turning on rock, or wheels turning on dirt, or the trailer itself starting to move . . .

Max ran to the window. He wasn't imagining that

part. The trailer *was* starting to move. In fact, it looked like the entire carnival was starting to move, that it had simply picked up stakes and the whole thing was moving. The big blue tent, the games, the Ferris wheel, everything was moving. *Maybe Tara had hypnotized him, too. No, he was certain that he heard it.* Wheels grinding on dirt, the sound of rocks crunching underneath, the landscape changing in a nanosecond, the landscape out the window almost a blur.

the runaway carnival

"Tess, Tess . . . Wake up." Max called out frantically as his sister was still lying motionless on the daybed.

Tess heard his voice almost as if it was coming through a tunnel.

"Tess, wake up! Please, Tess."

Tess tried to pull herself from sleep, *or was it sleep?* It was almost as if she was there but not there. She could hear his voice, but she couldn't open her eyes.

"Tess, wake up." He was shaking her now, and the warmth of his hands seemed to have an effect on her. She opened her eyes.

Tess must have been deeply asleep (or was she hypnotized?). Nothing looked exactly the same. Even the daylight seemed to have a different cast. Out the window there was a view of a grassy landscape and they seemed to be in full motion streaking past it and the passing sky was bright blue with white puffy clouds.

The sky in Devon that morning had been paler, almost blue-gray, lighter, more tranquil.

This was almost ultralight, as if the colors had been computer altered, brightened. Not quite DayGlo but very bright. And they were definitely moving as the sky and the grassy landscape continued to sweep by them or they continued to sweep by it . . .

"I think it's my fault," said Max, his voice wavering. "I think I've done something terrible." He ran back to the window and looked out, as if that was going to change anything.

"What do you mean?" asked Tess. "*What* could you have done?"

She stood up. She felt a little dizzy. She couldn't tell if she felt dizzy from being "hypnotized" or it was just because the trailer was rocking back and forth as it was moving quickly forward.

Tess ran unsteadily to the window where Max was standing, his eyes almost as big as saucers.

Where were they? It didn't look anything like Devon. Maybe she was still hypnotized.

Tess pinched herself. *No, she was definitely awake . . .* But where was Tara? They were alone in the trailer. Tess called out to her. "Tara?" But there wasn't any answer. "Is there another room in here?" she asked Max.

"I don't think so," said Max.

"Where's Tara?"

"I don't know," said Max. "I had my back turned to you and I was playing with the levers on the wall while she hypnotized you."

"What levers?" asked Tess.

"The levers and the steering wheel," he answered. "And the pulleys and the altitude lever . . ."

Tess gave him the oddest look. They both turned and looked at the front wall of the trailer, but it was absolutely flat. There weren't any levers, nothing that looked like a steering wheel, or an altitude control, or even a pulley. There wasn't anything like that. Just a plain, flat wall.

"Are you sure you weren't hypnotized, too," asked Tess, "and you might have imagined that?"

"Maybe," said Max. "But I don't think I'm imagining this . . ."

Max ran to the door and tried to open it. It wouldn't budge. It was as if it was sealed shut, like a door on an airplane or a spaceship.

Max tried to calculate how fast they were travelling from the view of the changing landscape outside, but there was no way to calibrate it. *It wasn't as if they were moving from tree to tree or town to town, or were they?* The images outside the window were almost a blur. *Maybe he was just still dizzy from the Ferris wheel? Or Tess was right, maybe he'd been hypnotized, too.* If that was true, he sort of hoped that he was going to wake up soon.

Then there was another giant noise, like the sound of a parking brake screeching to a halt on a hill or an anchor forcibly landing, as the trailer settled down with a thud.

Where were they?

There was something strange about the face of the hill they'd landed on: it wasn't rocky, quite the opposite. It was like a soft grassy slope, a rolling hill, with a similar rolling hill next to it and behind it, well, all around, really.

The color had backed off, so that the scenery was almost in watercolor now or fading.

There were a few evergreen trees in the distance and what looked like pine cones on the ground and an occasional patch of pale green moss. Max tried to remember his geography and whether there was an amazing mountain range in England. *Was there?* There were some rolling hills in Devon. Maybe they were still there.

There was no sign of Tara, who seemed to have completely disappeared. He didn't remember the door opening or her leaving. He just remembered that sound he'd heard of wheels turning on dirt, on rocks, as if the circus wagon was running away.

He wanted to call Aunt Evie. He wanted to tell her that they might be late . . . might not be at the brontosaurus at one thirty. He wanted to call his mom in Spain; even though she might not answer, at least he'd get through and hear her voice on her voicemail, which might be comforting, and leave her and their dad a message about where they were.

But where exactly were they?

The ground beneath them felt stable, constant, as if they weren't moving any more. Max frantically tried the door again. This time it opened.

*in which they wonder
if they're lost*

They didn't even speak. No comment from either of Max or Tess, just motion. Max was out the door first and Tess behind him, running headlong into the carnival, trying to make their way, or Max was anyway, to the outer gate.

Everything seemed to be g o i n g   s l o w e r. Tess couldn't quite explain that. The Ferris wheel didn't seem as fast. On the other hand, it had recently broken.

There was a pretzel stand where the cotton candy machine had been. Maybe they'd run the wrong direction and these were different food stands. The sign at the grill was advertising MEAT PIES instead of sausages. But the grill master looked a lot like Ben, the jolly fellow who'd sold Tess the candyfloss and called her "Missy" when she stepped off the Ferris wheel. MEAT PIES. Maybe that was something they sold later in the day, like a dinner entrée, Tess reasoned, trying to make sense of it. *Well, at least they were probably still in England. Maybe. Meat Pies.*

There was the blue tent. That was encouraging, and there was still the sign announcing the aerial ballet show with a painted poster. The poster had a picture of the three kids, a girl and boy who looked almost the same age, maybe twelve or thirteen years old and what must be their older sister, fourteen or fifteen. They were each hanging on to a bar, about to take off, in perfect position in the painting as if they were going to momentarily dance across the trapeze.

And there was still the sign that said:

THE BREATHTAKING BARANOVAS

Amazing Aerial Ballet Show!!
Starts promptly at 2:00 p.m.

Tess remembered that they'd promised Aunt Evie that they'd meet her at the brontosaurus at one thirty. *She wondered what time it was.* And that they'd bought tickets for the aerial ballet show. Everything was just the same, it was just the meat pies that had changed.

"Max!" she called out, but he kept running. Tess could definitely outrun him. "Max!" she exclaimed as she grabbed him by the arm. "Max! We promised Aunt Evie we'd meet her at one thirty. Wait. We're at the carnival. It's okay. See . . ." She made him turn around. "There's the picture of the aerial ballet. Just like there was before. See, at the blue tent. Calm down. I don't know what happened. But you know what Dad says about thinking before we act."

"Actually, that's what Dad says about you, not me," said Max.

"Well, in this case," said Tess sort of softly, trying to calm her brother down, not wanting him to get angry at her for saying it, "that probably apples to both of us. I mean, applies to both of us."

Max started laughing. "I kind of like 'apples to both of us,'" he said.

For some reason Tess couldn't explain, she thought it was funny, too. "Apples to both of us, then," she said. And they both started laughing.

After a minute, Tess said, "I think that we're supposed to take a beat here. Look at me, Max. We—we don't understand what happened and see," she said, "see that bench over there? We sat there. An hour ago? *Was it an hour ago?* Right when we got off the Ferris wheel and you had a lemonade and . . . and . . ." She couldn't explain what she was frightened of.

Rushing out of the carnival and not really knowing where they were? Not being able to get back in? Why did she think that was even a possibility? *Getting lost and not being able to get found?*

"You know what Dad says we should always remember," said Tess. "And you're better at this than me. Dad would say, 'Take a moment to assess the situation.' That's what he'd say."

She didn't say this next bit out loud. But their dad also said, "If you get lost, go back to where you started so that somebody could find you again." And they were presently surrounded by what seemed to Tess as significant markers.

The Ferris wheel *was* still there. They could see that. And off to the right, that funny roller coaster with biplanes as passenger vehicles. Each with the funny name.

"What time is it, Max?" asked Tess.

"I don't know," he answered.

He pulled his iPhone out of his pocket, but the screen had gone to black. Max pressed the power button . . . but nothing happened. He pressed it again. Still nothing. "I think it must've run out of battery. I knew I was supposed to charge it this morning."

"Let's use mine," said Tess. She pulled her phone out of her backpack, but it was turned off, too. *Or was it?* The screen was dark, really dark. She pushed the power button on *her* phone, but it didn't boot up, either.

"Did—you charge yours?" asked Max.

"I thought I did," said Tess. "But I don't know. The plug in the attic's kind of"—she searched for a word—"antique."

All Tess wanted in that moment was to be back in the attic room, the sound of the ocean outside, a soft, comforting rhythmic swell in the background, and Aunt Evie downstairs with seven kinds of yogurt in the fridge and . . .

She couldn't let Max know that she was afraid.

"Hey."

Tess turned to see who had spoken to her. She recognized him instantly. It was the boy in the poster, one of the Breathtaking Baranovas, who was standing in front of the poster, so that there couldn't be any mistaking who he was.

"Alexei," he said, before she'd even asked his name. "That was pretty impressive what you did," he said.

Tess had no idea what he was talking about. She was worried about Max, who had started running again toward the front gate.

"Max, hold up."

Max turned and looked at her and saw she was talking to that boy.

"Max, we have to stay together," Tess yelled out. Max turned around and walked back to her.

"My sister and I were watching you in horror," Alexei said, "when you saved that little boy."

That seemed so long ago—the Ferris wheel ride.

"Oh," said Tess, somewhat modestly. She thought it was a good sign that Alexei had seen that happen.

"We were," he almost stammered, "we were kind of worried about you," he said.

"I guess I didn't think much before I jumped," said Tess. "And then I didn't breathe much until I caught him, and eased him back in his seat, and shut the chariot door. And then," she confessed, looking a little pale when she said this, "I looked—down for a minute."

"You're never supposed to look down," said Alexei.

"I know that," said Tess. "That's what I always tell

Max because he gets motion sickness and I'm always scared he's going to get dizzy. *Don't look down.* But there I was, up in the air, and I could hear people screaming at me from below . . ."

"Applauding, you mean. Everyone was clapping," said Alexei. "And cheering!"

"It just sounded like screaming," said Tess.

"It *was* pretty impressive," said Tatiana. She was Alexei's sister, actually his twin, and she'd joined him outside the tent. "It was jaw-droppingly impressive," she said. "I mean, we could have done it, but we're trained." She had a funny attitude when she said this. And Tess wondered what the girl really thought of her.

"I'm Tess," said Tess.

The girl answered, "I'm Tatiana."

Of course she would have a name like Tatiana, thought Tess, *an over-the-top, theatrical name.* But she was ashamed that she'd thought that. They were both Russian and those were perfectly reasonable names for two children who were from Russia: Tatiana and Alexei.

"We're twins," Tatiana said.

"I thought you might be," said Max. "I'm Max, Tess's brother." He reached his hand out politely to take hers.

Tatiana didn't quite shake it actually. It was more like

the way a royal princess would take someone's hand when it had been offered to her. *Or were you never supposed to offer your hand to royalty?* Tess couldn't remember. And she was quite sure Max wasn't aware if there was a rule or not.

"Have you ever trained in aerial ballet?" Tatiana asked Tess, quite seriously.

"No," said Tess, laughing. "I dance a bit. I've always wanted to though, secretly, dance on a trapeze." And she added, kind of wistfully, "I imagined I did once. I think that's what it was. But I've always wanted to really fly, I mean try."

"Fly," said Tatiana, repeating Tess's mistake. "That sounds like one of those mistakes you make, when you mean to say one thing and you actually say what you mean to say by mistake."

"A Freudian slip," said Max. "Is that what you mean?"

"We don't like to use the word 'slip,'" said Tatiana, "in aerial ballet," showing that she, too, almost had a sense of humor.

"I'm glad we found you," said Tess. "We thought we were lost."

"Oh, yes," said Alexei, sounding very serious when he said it. "We were wondering when you were going to get to that part . . ."

inside the blue tent

Tess looked at Alexei for the longest time. He hadn't really answered her question. There was an awkward silence before he said, "It's still an hour before the show," said Alexei. "Do you want to see the stage and the aerial trapeze?"

Max interrupted him. "You know what time it is," said Max.

"Of course," said Alexei.

That was reassuring.

"We have to keep track of time when we have a show to do," he explained. "There's nothing scheduled before us and we always like to do a little warm-up before the show. *Do* you want to see it?" he asked.

"I do," said Tess emphatically, looking at Max and hoping he would agree. Max nodded.

"Touch the sky," said Alexei and then he did the strangest thing.

He put his hand up against the seemingly enclosed tent. The fabric of the tent practically looked as thin as a balloon except it was made of the finest parachute silk, blue and shimmery. And right where Alexei put his index finger, pointed it almost like a wand, it was as if a sharp knife came down and slit the tent and created an opening as if it had been a curtain all along.

Alexei held a side of it open for Tess, Max, and Tatiana to enter. Then he entered himself, and there was the funniest sound like a high-tech zipper, as the tent seemed to close itself up behind them as if there'd never been an entrance at all.

Tess did think that was sort of curious.

There were bleachers, tiered so that the back row was higher than the front row, the seats and rows all lined in a semicircle, almost like a theater in the round. There was a silvery white moon painted on the top of the tent and a brilliant splash of sparkling stars. *Tess wondered how painted stars could sparkle.* And then she remembered the sparkling stars on the ceiling of the psychic wagon.

"Special effect," said Max as if he'd read her mind. "It's probably electric."

But Tess continued to look up. She was mesmerized by the elaborate array of swings, bars, multileveled platforms, and the bright-silver tightrope, taut as steel, strung in a strange geometric pattern, connecting all of the acrobatic equipment in the air emphasized by the backdrop of sparkling stars.

"Do *you* want to try it?" Tatiana asked Tess. There was something vaguely taunting in the way she said it, almost as if it was "a dare"!

"More than anything," said Tess, completely forgetting in that moment that, especially in England, it was sometimes a good idea to be careful what you wish for.

If they were still in England, that is, since really nobody had quite answered that question yet.

Alexei was already halfway up one of the silk rope ladders on the right of the stage, climbing to a top platform. Tatiana pointed Tess to a ladder on the other side.

"Don't worry," Tatiana said, "I'll be right behind you." Tess started to scramble up but looked down at her jeans and worried she might be at a disadvantage.

"Hold on," said Tatiana, and ran to get a pair of tights and a leotard for Tess and a pair of silver ballet slippers that tied in a criss-cross up the leg.

She showed Tess a small dressing room, really just another curtain off to the side, and Tess slipped her clothes off and changed into the tights, the leotard, and the silver ballet slippers, which fit her perfectly, almost as if they'd been made for her.

Tess noticed that the leotard itself had silver stars sewn into it and they sparkled, sort of the way the stars did on the ceiling. Tess wasn't sure what to make of that—maybe it was paint with glitter in it? She realized the stars were appliqué patches as one of them, the one right by her right hip, was coming loose. She started to play with it, to see if she could get it to stick, but it was actually sewn on.

"I think it becomes you," a voice behind her said. Tess recognized it instantly, soft, almost hypnotic. The voice of Tara, the psychic. "Are you losing a star?" The word *star* was elongated, almost as if there was more than one *rrr* at the end of it. "I can help with that," she said. "It's never a good idea to lose a star," said Tara, whispering, as if there was more meaning to it than just a piece of a ballet costume coming loose. "Let me sew it on for you," she said. "There's lots of silk thread here."

Tess tried to see where Tara had appeared from, as she hadn't seen anyone else in the tent when they entered . . . but then again Tess had been behind the curtain getting dressed . . .

"This looks like a perfect color," said Tara, holding up a spool of silver thread. "But I don't see a needle anywhere . . . That's irritating, I don't even see a sewing kit."

"Curiously enough," said Tess, "I have one, I think."

Tess reached down for her jeans, which she'd hastily folded on the floor, and carefully pulled from the right front pocket the silver needle and, without even thinking, handed it to Tara. "Will this do?"

"Oh, yes," said Tara, her voice soft and melodic again. "I think it will do very nicely." The needle sparkled a bit, but everything was sparkling silver, too, so Tess didn't think much of it.

There were so many questions Tess wanted to ask. *Where were they? Had the carnival picked up stakes and moved?* Or had she and Max imagined it all.

But Tess could hear that the music was starting and the clock was ticking down for any practice time before Alexei and Tatiana's performance. And her chance at aerial ballet. So, Tess simply did as she was told.

"Hold very still," Tara said to Tess. "I think that we can do this quickly."

The needle seemed to sparkle again as Tara threaded it, in one quick aim, with the tip of the silver thread she'd expertly moistened with her tongue, as if she was a professional seamstress.

"Hold very very still," she said to Tess.

Tess took a perfect ballerina pose, shoulders back, head up, as Tara pulled the fabric of the leotard ever so slightly away from Tess's body so that she could, without poking Tess with the needle, firmly reattach the star.

"There," she said, after three or four very careful stitches. "I think that will hold.

"Now, let's fix your hair," said Tara. "This will only take a moment. I'm very good at updos."

It was such a funny word, sort of like a word Aunt Evie would use.

"You probably think I mean a ballerina bun," said Tara, shaking her head. "But I was thinking something much more dramatic."

Tara opened her left hand and revealed three silver hairpins crested with three diamonds each. "After all," said Tara, "it's very special to have a chance to dance in the sky."

Tess stood perfectly still again as Tara swept Tess's long brown hair up, in one quick motion, folding it into a high French twist, and perfectly pinned it with the three clips.

She turned Tess around, almost like she was a doll, and pointed her to a three-paneled mirror. Tara turned one side of the mirror, so Tess could see both her front and her back. "Voila, updo," said Tara, "Very spectacular, don't you think?"

Tess almost didn't recognize herself. It wasn't that she looked older, but her cheekbones were more defined, her neck thin and graceful. She looked elegant somehow, as if she was out of another century, an earlier century, for sure.

Tara hadn't applied any makeup but it looked as if Tess had some on. *Maybe it was the lighting.* Her eyes seemed to be outlined in the finest dark kohl, her eyelashes curled and also darkened, her skin pale but her cheeks lightly flushed, as if she *was* wearing blush, and she swore it looked as if she had lipstick on. It had to be the lighting, or lack of lighting maybe, as she realized there wasn't any lighting in the tiny curtained dressing room.

Tess wished her mom was there to see her, and her dad, and Aunt Evie. But she quickly remembered that she wasn't sure they would totally approve of a lesson in aerial ballet . . . She pushed that thought aside, although she did remember that her mom had nixed that trampoline course she'd wanted to take in Greenwich Village when she was eight. This was different, she reasoned, these were real professionals. Actual Aerial Ballet Stars.

Alexei was up on the top platform already. He was swinging a bar back and forth, pushing it away, then catching it almost as if he was playing ball, casually with one hand, so relaxed, as if he was oblivious to the fact that he was on a platform high up off the ground.

Tatiana hadn't waited for Tess, after all. She had climbed up to a middle platform. She was standing on her hands, her body as straight as a board, as confidently as anyone else could stand on their feet, except she was standing on *one* hand.

Tess had a sense she was about to be outclassed. Tess could do a one-handed cartwheel. Multiple one-handed cartwheels, in fact. It had sometimes been her preferred way of crossing the living room when she was five, multiple cartwheels, to her mother's delight and sometimes horror. But Tess was certain she couldn't do a one-handed handstand, not without a month (or a year) of practice, and certainly not when she was sixty-five feet up in the air . . . with the distinct possibility of looking down without even meaning to. Impressive and somewhat terrifying.

Tess reassured herself. There *was* a big net down at the bottom below the trapeze that also curiously sparkled a bit. It looked as if it, too, was made out of spun silk. Tess was certain it was strong enough to catch her if she fell. And gentle enough to fall into so that it would feel almost like falling into a cushion. Well, it might hurt a bit, but at least it would catch her.

She watched as Tatiana executed a double flip in the air and landed perfectly on the platform on two feet and then pointed to Tess that it was her turn to climb up the silk ladder. The way Tatiana pointed to her really felt like a dare. Tess reminded herself that she wasn't normally afraid of dares. Her first response was usually, *Okay, watch this, then.*

Tess put one silver-ballet-slippered foot onto the first rung of the silk ladder, balancing so that the rung was under the arch of her foot, and her heel and toe were pointed around it. She pulled herself up with one hand grasping one side of the ladder.

The ladder started to swing with her weight. That didn't bother her at all. Tess just leaned in and started to sway with the music that was playing in the background, classical music, sort of, violins, or maybe just one violin, and big brassy horns, with a deep bass drumbeat. It sounded kind of like hip-hop meets classical, if there was such a thing, incredibly easy to dance to or, in the present circumstances, incredibly comfortable to swing to.

There was a long drumbeat, which Tess took as a cue. She pointed her left foot daintily up onto the next rung, then did the same again, balancing on her instep. Then, began to climb the ladder quickly, scaling it almost, never having both of her feet touch the same rung of the ladder at the same time. She continued to climb, higher and higher, scaling with her arms, as well, one after the other. She added a couple of ballet-like arm gestures, too, holding a hand to her waist and lifting her elbow, then grabbing the ladder with that hand and putting her other hand above her head as if she was about to do a pirouette.

She reached the top of the ladder and couldn't help it, she set her right hand down on the platform and executed a one-handed cartwheel, nailed the landing perfectly, her head straight up, her shoulders back, and her arms gently out almost in a circle, with her hands clasped in front of her in a perfect ballerina stance.

Out of the corner of her eye, she saw Alexei smile at her, and turned to Tatiana, who was smiling in approval, too.

She had a feeling she was going to like this.

a dance in the sky

Don't look down. That's the first rule. Tess knew that.

Instead she looked across at Alexei, who was swinging the bar more intently now, catching it with one hand, throwing it with both, catching it again. He stood poised, as if on a diving board, his back totally straight, his eyes focused straight ahead, but Tess couldn't tell on what, perhaps the view of the silver bar as it came into view just at his sightline.

He gripped the bar with two hands and flew, swinging as if it was the most natural thing in the world, hanging by his hands, and then, almost turning himself into a circle, slipped his legs over the bar and bent them. For a moment, he sat on the bar as straight as if it was a dining chair, then he swung around and he was hanging, holding on by his knees. His head was down and his arms were swinging back and forth as if he had a mind to catch someone. He turned and looked at Tess.

Alexei smiled at her, almost as if he was teasing her. Then turned toward his sister Tatiana, who was casually swinging a bar back and forth herself, catching it and tossing it away, from her place on the platform across the stage.

A drumbeat sounded insistently. Tatiana grabbed the bar firmly with two hands, pointed her toes, and swung off the platform, as if she was flying through the air. Once, twice, back and forth, and then she let go of her bar, executed a triple somersault in the air, and landed perfectly holding Alexei's hands, who was still swinging by his knees on the other bar. And the two of them were swinging together, in such synchronicity, almost as if they were one body, dancing through the air.

Tess thought she heard applause from the bleachers

below. But she didn't look down to see if there was anyone there. *Don't look down.*

Alexei and Tatiana continued to swing.

Then Tatiana executed a jump through the air, turned one somersault, and landed perfectly in a hollow circle that lit up magically at one end of the trapeze. A full spotlight shining directly on it. Or maybe it was back-lit? A white sphere that appeared shaded on one side, bright white, shaped like a crescent moon inside the circle with a perfect lilt at the bottom, which was a seat for Tatiana to rest on, which she did, with a lot of attitude and grace. And once seated, she crossed her leg and pointed her toe.

Tess thought that was funny—it was sort of like the man in the moon, except it was the woman in the moon. She wondered who had thought that up. She was certain she heard more applause, screams of delight, and "Ahhs," from below. She didn't think she was imagining it. But Tess didn't look down.

Alexei was looking at her now.

He swung a bar over to her. Tess noticed it was hanging from braided silver satin ropes. She reached casually, but missed as if she hadn't meant to catch it, or she wasn't so easy to catch, and let it fly back through the air to him. Alexei caught it again with two fingers, almost as if he was showing off or taunting her to perform. He swung it back to her. She stood and simply stared at him and didn't even try to catch it. She heard people laughing below—she was sure of it—as if they appreciated her performance.

Alexei caught it again. And before he threw it back again, he whispered, strangely as if it was coming through a microphone and Tess alone could hear it, "Touch the sky."

Alexei swung the bar back to her. This time, Tess pointed her toes, as if she was about to dive off a diving board, and with the tips of her fingers as if she'd done this a hundred times before, grasped the bar and folded her hands tightly around it, and pushed off, propelling herself forward, and literally flew through the air still pointing her toes as she did so, feeling her own momentum as she swung gracefully and seemingly effortlessly from the bar.

Casually, Tatiana, who was still in a sitting position on the moon, gently threw another flying bar to Tess.

Was Tess supposed to catch this? She let it fly. She effected the same attitude she had before, as if she was simply ignoring the swinging bar as she let it fly back to Tatiana. Tatiana caught it again and swung it back to her. Tess ignored it again. Tatiana caught and swung it back to her.

Tess was ready this time. She effected a somersault right through the air and flew to catch the second bar and missed . . .

Flat out missed.

There was a deep cry from the crowd as . . .

Tess started to go into a free fall, except she realized she didn't have a parachute. Falling, falling downward. Was there a net below her? She was frightened to look. There'd been a net when she first went up. And then the thing she didn't want to think about—could a net really save her if she was falling too hard, fast, with such velocity that she wouldn't stop until she hit the ground? Deep breath. She caught Alexei's eye, as if his stare alone was something to hold on to.

Everything in that moment became crisp and clear. And it seemed, for a moment, as if she was in a slow fall, or time itself had slowed down, and the space around her expanding, giving her a way to reassess, regain her balance, if only there was something there to balance on.

Falling. She heard Alexei's voice. Was he calling to her? Or was she just remembering? "Touch the sky."

Something was sticking into her hip sharply. She reached down, right around the star that Tara had resewn onto her costume, and she touched the needle, which Tara had carelessly left still threaded into her leotard. It was the sharp point of the needle digging into Tess's skin right by her hip. She started to pull it away . . .

As Tess's hand touched the bright silver needle, it was almost as if there were sparks and she was encased in a halo of light. Red, blue, yellow, silver, purple, green, all the colors of the rainbow surrounding her. *Were they spotlights or was it coming from the silver needle?* Tess didn't know.

But for a moment, it was as though time had frozen and given her a chance to make a move.

Instinctively she turned her body into a somersault again, the way a high diver would, one and a half turns as if she'd jumped from a diving board and done it on purpose. As if somehow the act of tumbling would slow her fall.

The voices in the crowd below flared up into "oohs" and "ahhs."

There wasn't a crowd below her, was there? Tess didn't know. She knew she wasn't allowed to look down.

Cascading around her was a super-spray of lights, as if there were twenty spotlights on, each coming from a different angle and in varying rainbow colored shades. She held the needle up. And wondered again, as it was so much like a Fourth of July sparkler, she questioned where the light was coming from.

Then, almost as if by magic, a swing dropped down, held by silver ropes. The seat of the swing was pink satin and it had thickness that was comforting to see.

There was a way that she could navigate there if she really tried. It was almost right below her to the right. Tess flipped into the last half turn, and listed as far as she could to the right, and landed, as if it had been rehearsed, played out, exactly meant to be, perfectly in the seat of the swing. She caught the ropes and held on tightly with her hands, and crossed her legs, pointing her toes triumphantly, the way a ballerina would, as if it had been all part of the act, after all.

The crowd below burst into cheers. Hurrahs, whistles, screams of delight and fancy. Tess sailed softly in the air, secure in the swing, gently, almost as if she was in a playground. As she swung gracefully and softly through the air, she looked down as the crowd rose up in a standing ovation and she realized the audience was sold-out, packed house, standing room only, and everyone was standing, and she had been part of the act, after all.

after the show

Were you trying to upstage me?" asked Tatiana, mock teasing Tess, smiling when she said it. "That was a little close there, though, wasn't it?"

Tess just smiled back. Her heart was racing. Pounding really. She could feel every muscle in her body, aching, not in pain, just keyed up as if ready to be in motion, each part still completely in sync with each other as if she had to make another move, or wanted to, if they were to do an encore or she had to take another bow.

There had been two "curtain calls." There wasn't a curtain really, but the audience whooped and applauded so loudly they went back on stage again. The sound itself was exhilarating. Strange to be the one up on stage in a big arena. And have all those people applauding you. After three bows and a triple cartwheel by Tatiana, which Tess wisely didn't try to replicate, they left the stage. The crowd still wouldn't settle down. And they went back on stage. Tess wondered if they were supposed to do an encore, but Alexei, as if he'd read her mind, shook his head. And taking the middle spot, took Tatiana's hand in his right and Tess's in the left and they all bowed again, in perfect unison this time, as if they were actually joined at the hip.

Someone threw a bouquet of white roses onto the stage at Tess's feet. She looked at Tatiana, who nodded her assent, and Tess picked them up and held them in her arms. She realized it was someone connected to the carnival who had tossed them. She could tell by the way he stood, surveying everything, sort of like he owned the place. And there was something about the way he was looking at Tess that gave her pause. She graciously handed the flowers to

Tatiana. The crowd cheered even more loudly, as if they respected her humility, her ability to share. But the crowd didn't know what she knew. She knew that she'd flat out missed and for some almost inexplicable reason been given a second chance.

"Brilliant," said Alexei, not hiding the respect and awe in his voice. Their eyes locked again for a moment. And Tess wanted to tell him how much he'd helped her, but she was too shy.

She was also exhilarated. Was her heart beating from the "ride"? It had been a ride. Or was she just so proud of herself and, frankly, a little bit impressed with herself? It wasn't as if she was about to get a swelled head. It had been much too scary for that. Too close a call, so to speak. But it had been totally amazing. It was going to take her a minute to calm down. She felt as if she was still flying.

"We've never seen that happen before, have we, Alexei?" said Tatiana.

"Seen what?" asked Max.

Tess knew what they were talking about.

"The swing," said Tatiana.

"It must be new," said Alexei. "Good thing somebody thought to drop it down."

"Is that what you think it was?" asked Tara, who was in

the dressing room helping them change. "A new prop that somebody dropped from the sky?"

"Yes," said Alexei and Tatiana together.

Max started to say something, but Tess interrupted him. She looked at Tara so strangely. "What was it, then?" asked Tess.

Tara blinked her eyes, the way she did when she knew something that others didn't, even though the answer to Tara was sometimes quite obvious. Looking at Tess she said, "I think you would call it"—she hesitated—"Carnival Magic."

an encounter
with lorenzo

Tess's cheeks were flushed, her heart still racing, over-excited, slightly enthused when she walked out of the blue tent back onto the grounds of the carnival. She'd actually performed in an aerial ballet show. In the back of her mind, though, she realized that if there had been a crowd, there was a crowd, and she'd actually performed, it must be after two. She didn't mention this to Max. Not yet anyway. She realized she couldn't see, from any

angle, the brontosaurus anywhere. Was Aunt Evie waiting for them somewhere else? Had the carnival actually
moved? She couldn't remember if she'd seen the brontosaurus after they'd first left the psychic wagon.

Max, meanwhile, noticed that the sun was starting to
go down in the sky. Not setting yet. But it was getting late
in the day. The carnival seemed less crowded. He wondered what time it really was. He realized Aunt Evie, by
now, must be hysterical. It was later than one thirty. He
couldn't see the brontosaurus ride. Max didn't tell this to
Tess because he didn't want to scare her, either. Max realized he needed a minute to think. Logically. Sort this all
out so that it sort of made sense. He felt as if it was all his
fault. He'd pulled the levers and played with the steering
wheel, if there'd been a steering wheel. He was sure there
was and that it had started to spin . . . He tried to remember
his dad's advice: *Take a moment to assess the situation.*

He didn't realize the situation might move so fast there
might not be time to assess it.

Tess announced that she was thirsty. Tatiana and Alexei
walked them over to the meat pie stand so Tess could get
a glass of water, but their way was blocked by a tall, mus-
cular man wearing a white T-shirt. The man who'd tossed
the roses to Tess. The sleeves of his T-shirt had been

purposefully ripped to expose his built-up biceps and a tattoo on his right arm that said THRILL RIDERS in an elaborate cursive scroll. There was a symbol underneath that was like a musical clef turned on its side. His name, they learned, was Lorenzo Leone, and he was the owner of the carnival.

"Oh," he said, "it's the girl who can fly through the stars."

He had a faint Italian accent. His tone was menacing (although Tess couldn't quite explain why) and complimentary at the same time. It felt like an encounter with the Vice Principal in the hallway at your school when you were definitely the person she was looking for and you didn't know yet if you'd done something bad or something good—like, kind of, it could go either way.

There was no getting around him. Alexei and Tatiana didn't even try, and neither did Tess or Max. He had another man with him, who was also scary but in a different way. His name was Isaac, but everyone called him Izzy. He was shorter than Lorenzo, red-faced, bald, also tattooed, a slinky large green lizard right up his right arm. He looked like he could throw a mean punch if he was given even the slightest opportunity.

"Hi, I'm Max," said Max, sticking his hand out

politely to Lorenzo, "and this is my sister, Tess," he added, so at least Lorenzo would know that they were polite and didn't mean to do anyone any harm or interfere in any way. *In fact, all they really wanted was to go home.* Home in this case would be Aunt Evie's beach cottage, which Max hoped was just a little ways away, down the mountain, by the sea, where they'd started out to begin with . . .

Lorenzo just nodded to him. Max felt somewhat foolish holding his hand out to someone who wouldn't take it. But Max wisely understood that that might have more to do with Lorenzo's character than his own.

This wasn't something their dad had ever said, but it would be something Max would say to their dad if he ever had a chance: *Never trust anyone who won't shake your hand.*

welcome to the carnival

Excellent performance, my dear," Lorenzo said to Tess.

Tess looked at him somewhat suspiciously before she answered, "Thanks."

"I've been looking for someone exactly like you," said Lorenzo. "Welcome aboard."

It sounded like something a pirate would say: "Welcome aboard." Lorenzo smiled, and that was sort of reminiscent of a cartoon version of a pirate, too, as when he smiled he revealed a silver tooth just to the left of his bottom front teeth, which seemed to glisten in a somewhat menacing way.

"What do you think, kids?" he asked, looking at Alexei and Tatiana. "The Breathtaking Baranovas were a better act when there were three of you!" He held up three fingers cheerfully.

"That's not our doing," said Tatiana brazenly, with just a hint of sadness underneath the anger. She pointed at him. "*You're* the one who sent our sister away."

"That I did," Lorenzo said, as if he was almost proud of it. "One of the best deals I've ever made."

"But you said, Lorenzo," Alexei said firmly, "that it was only for a little while. That you were just loaning her out for a little while, to that other carnival, to star in their show! And . . ."

Tatiana weighed in, too, the way she and Alexei had of finishing sentences for each other. "You promised," she said, "you promised, you promised . . ."

"We miss her," they both said together. "It isn't the same without our sister Anna. We miss her every minute of every day."

"I miss her, too," said Lorenzo, laughing again as if he had a secret. "Apparently, she's a box-office sensation."

He said this last word almost as if it had spaces between the syllables: "sen-sa-tion." "Absolutely miraculous," he said. "They've just extended her contract and offered me, I mean her, a big raise."

Max wondered whether this was just a slip of the tongue. How much money was Lorenzo making off Tatiana and Alexei's sister Anna?

"But isn't it a miracle, too," asked Lorenzo, looking Tess up and down in a way she really didn't like, as if she was a prize-winning thoroughbred racehorse or something. "Isn't it a miracle," he repeated, "that Tess has come to the carnival? And, now there are going to be three of you again! And everyone would agree, her first performance was sen-sa-tional. Do you think you can do that again, dear?" Lorenzo asked, laughing. "Of course you can."

Tess wasn't sure she could do that again, at all.

There was something about the whole encounter that made Tess afraid to respond. Her normal response would have been: *Isn't this something you're supposed to ask me if I want to do?* But she had a feeling the answer to that was going to be "No," and if that was the case, it was probably better just to be quiet. It was one of the things her dad had taught her. "It's always best to choose your battles," he'd said to Tess, and then he'd added, "and try not to pick the ones you can't win."

"I have a job for you, too, Sonny," Lorenzo said, laughing, looking at Max, his silver tooth even more visible when he laughed.

But before either Tess or Max could even respond to him, Lorenzo disappeared into The House of Mirrors that they hadn't even noticed they were standing next to before.

But Lorenzo didn't disappear into the entrance. It was almost as if he'd walked straight through one of the mirrored walls of glass itself and simply disappeared, leaving behind a somewhat ghostly laugh that seemed to reverberate through the air.

they start to understand
there might not really
be a way to get away

"You'll stay with us tonight," said Tatiana, who had been quietly watching the whole thing.

"What do you mean?" said Max. "We want to go home."

Max couldn't imagine what Aunt Evie would think if they didn't go home. He pushed the thought away.

But Tess said it out loud. "What do you think Aunt Evie will think if we don't come home tonight? What do you think she would do? She has to be half hysterical by now. And . . . and . . ." Tess was close to tears, which was very much unlike her. "We want to go home. Why can't we go home?"

"We'd like you to go home, too," said Alexei, who was standing behind her. "Not because we don't want you here. Don't think that. But because we know that's what you and Max want to do. But you can't go home," said Alexei. "Not yet, anyway. There isn't really a way to go home."

"That's ridiculous," said Max. Even though the logical part of his brain was tending to believe Alexei. "We can just walk out the gate and . . ."

"No," said Tatiana. "The carnival's closed, and there isn't really a gate to walk out of . . . not in the sense that you mean . . . Not for us anyway, not once you become one of the carnival workers."

"But *I'm* not a carnival worker," said Max.

"Yes, you are," said Tatiana. She said each word distinctly, as if there was a beat between. As if something had happened and he had been transformed.

Max looked down at his clothes and saw that inexplicably he was wearing old-fashioned overalls with a long-sleeved shirt underneath. The sneakers he'd had on had been replaced by black lace-up work boots that were comfortable but didn't look at all familiar. He had a funny scarf tied at his neck that was red-and-white checked. He didn't own a scarf like that. In fact, he didn't own any cotton or silk scarves at all, just woolen ones for winter.

"Yes, you are," said Tatiana and Alexei, quite definitively and frighteningly in tandem. "You already are."

Tess wondered if this was somehow her fault. If when she'd agreed to take the aerial ballet lesson, she'd somehow signed them up.

Max wondered whether it was his fault. When he'd played with the levers and the steering wheel—he was certain there'd been a steering wheel there—that somehow they'd gone on a ride of some kind that they couldn't get off.

Lorenzo suddenly appeared again, out of The House of Mirrors, almost like a ghost himself, since his face was reflected in the mirror and another mirror and another mirror and so on. "You," he said.

Max looked behind him to see who Lorenzo was talking to. "No, you," said Lorenzo.

"Me?" asked Max a little sheepishly.

"What'd you say your name was, kid, 'Martin'?"

"No, Max," said Max.

"Oh, Max. That's easier. It's shorter. Sorta like you, kid. Ha ha." Lorenzo laughed out loud. "Max, or should I call you 'Shorty'? You come with me. Lemme show you the entrance to The House of Mirrors. I have just the job for you."

Max didn't understand what he could do that would be helpful at The House of Mirrors. He didn't look scary. Wasn't The House of Mirrors supposed to be a little scary? And isn't there always that funny mirror where you look very strange? He wondered if there *was* that mirror at the end that distorts the way a person's reflection looks in the mirror, very tall, at first and then you look round and very short. All mooshed out, so to speak.

Max thought the only part of this that applied to him was, he was pretty short. At least an inch shorter than Tess. And Tess was barely five foot one.

Max's dad had been promising him he'd have a growth spurt. He told Max he was short, too, when he was his age—now, he was six foot one—but Max didn't believe it. He'd accustomed himself to being a little short.

His mom had told him to use it as an advantage. He was complaining to her about his soccer playing and that a lot of the other kids were taller than he was and his mom had said, "That's your advantage, Max. You're a surprise."

Max took that advice to heart in more than one way. *That was his advantage. He was a surprise.* He wondered if he'd have the opportunity to ever show Lorenzo what a surprise he could be.

"Okay, cone of silence, kid," said Lorenzo when they got to the front entrance of The House of Mirrors. "Promise. Not a word to anyone. Got it?" His voice was pretty menacing.

"Got it," said Max, although he didn't know what he "got" yet.

"There's this thing that happens, see," said Lorenzo. "Sometimes, sometimes, well, people get a little bit freaked out in The House of Mirrors, especially if they turn the wrong way, hit a dead end, you know. And then they just see a reflection of themselves over and over and over again, and, like, they get kind of nervous, frightened, panicky . . . I don't know why that would freak anyone out. I like seeing myself in multiples," Lorenzo said. "I think it's, umm, y'know, powerful." He stretched out the word "power-ful" so it definitely had three syllables and lasted a long time when he said it. Max knew better than to respond to this. He just nodded.

"Anyway," said Lorenzo, "sometimes this other thing happens . . . I don't know how to explain it. Maybe it's too hot in there or something. Too many reflecting lights." The word "toooo" was pronounced as if the *o*s were three syllables long.

"Sometimes," Lorenzo said, "people see something else in The House of Mirrors. Something that they think is scary. Sorta like a"—he hesitated—"ghost sighting. But it's an image of another . . . I can't even explain it. I think they ate too much chocolate or something." His voice deepened, and the words seemed to echo as if it scared him, too. He spoke this next part slowly and clearly and quite definitively. "They see an image," he said, "of another carnival reflected on the other side of the glass. It's always in black-and-white and there's a feeling when you see it, like maybe you could step into the mirror and never return." His voice got really spooky at this point. "It's old-fashioned and frightening . . . Of course I've never seen it," said Lorenzo, speaking quite quickly again.

Max wondered if that was true. There was something dark and disturbing about Lorenzo's description and the way his voice sounded when he got to the part about "stepping into the mirror" that made Max think Lorenzo might have seen it, too.

"Anyway, kid," said Lorenzo, "sometimes when this thing happens, someone in The House of Mirrors will start to scream. I mean scream, scream, scream," he said three times for emphasis, "without even stopping to catch a breath. We know it's scary in there sometimes, but when this happens," and he handed Max a very big pocket watch that wasn't set up like a regular clock at all, "the clock'll start ticking . . ."

"By itself," asked Max, always practical, "or do I have to do something to it?"

"No, the clock just starts ticking by itself. I had it specially made."

Max looked at the face of the clock and realized it only had seven minutes on it. That was curious.

"And when it gets to six and a half minutes . . ." said Lorenzo.

"That's an awfully long time to let someone scream," said Max.

"It's a carnival, kid, no one really notices. But when it gets to six and a half minutes, a bell's going to go off and you're going to run as fast as you can into The House of Mirrors. I'm going to show you the way. And you're going to find whoever's screaming. There's a secret exit, which I'm going to show you in the morning. And you, Max, are going to lead them out, as if nothing whatsoever has happened. It's all in their head. You got it, kiddo, it's all in their head. If they got a kid with them, you get a candy-floss on the house immediately and free iced tea for the grown-ups.

"You do what I tell you, kid," said Lorenzo. "No one should be afraid at Lorenzo's Fun Fair."

Max didn't say anything. He didn't want Lorenzo to know that he and Tess might be scared. That was another lesson their dad had taught him. *Never let anyone know if you're scared.*

"Knew you were a smart kid," said Lorenzo. "I'm going to give you some advice. It's a good idea to stay on my good side." Max, who was a smart kid, had already figured that out.

the first sleepover at the runaway carnival

They called it their "apartment" as a joke. Alexei and Tatiana lived in a tent. It was a mini-version of the big blue tent. Really mini—barely as big as a tent you might find on a roadside campsite. They had offered to share it with Tess and Max.

"There's room for four of us, almost. Three of us used to sleep there, anyway," said Tatiana, making a reference to their sister, "and I'm sure we can squish in one more."

Alexei added, "I don't think you want to sleep by yourselves up here."

"Up where?" said Max.

"Well, usually we go to France after England and do a tour of Provence, which is very beautiful," said Tatiana, "but sometimes Lorenzo gets lonely for the Italian Alps, so this year that was the next stop. I think he was born here."

"The Italian Alps?" said Tess, making it also sound like a question.

Max and Tess's dad had talked to them a lot about how different a mountain or a desert can look, depending on where it's located. He said, for example, that the desert in New Mexico was very pink sometimes and that the Sahara Desert was startlingly white.

"The Italian Alps," Tess said again, but this time it sounded less like a question.

Tess tried to picture it in her mind. She and Max had gone to boarding school the year before in the Swiss Alps. She had to admit that the countryside around them, what they could see of it anyway, as they were still surrounded by carnival attractions, did look sort of like the Alps. There were some big pine trees visible in the distance and the soft slope of a mountain behind them, which

Tess imagined in winter might be a perfect kids' ski slope. She wondered if there was a chocolate store in the town, wherever the town might be, and if the ice cream was as splendid and extra creamy as it had been in Switzerland. But then she stopped herself.

What was she thinking? They were in Devon. In Devon-by-the-Sea. And Aunt Evie would be there at one thirty meeting them at the brontosaurus. That's what they'd arranged. The brontosaurus at one thirty. The brontosaurus...

Tess realized it was long past one thirty. It was night-time. And she realized she hadn't seen a glimpse of the brontosaurus ride since, well, she wasn't sure since when—since the aerial ballet stint, for sure . . .

The air around them had a distinct chill. It was as crisp and clear as the air in the Swiss Alps. Maybe that was just what nighttime was like in Devon; she reasoned they hadn't been there long enough to make a complete determination. But there was not a hint of moisture or a sea breeze in the air. Not a trace. There were stars twinkling brightly in the sky, which was midnight blue, and there was a perfect half-moon. Tess couldn't remember what that meant. If there was a meaning to a half-moon—an old legend or a warning. She couldn't remember.

All she knew was that she and Max were about to bunk in with Tatiana and Alexei for the night. She wondered what Aunt Evie might be thinking and if she'd called their parents yet.

"You know you can't leave, don't you?" said Tara to Tess quietly, as they were trailing behind the others walking up the hill towards the tent. "That if you step outside the gates," she added, "you won't be where you think you are. But you already figured that out, didn't you, Tess?"

Tess nodded.

Tess tried to reassure herself that she was imagining all of this. Like she was so scared, she'd become paranoid or something, and Tara hadn't just whispered that to her.

Tess tried to pretend it was just a sleepover, that they'd been invited to camp out. It had been Tara's idea that they bunk in with Alexei and Tatiana. *But should she trust Tara? Was something else going to happen in the middle of the night?*

Tara had already prepared the tent, turned down the beds, so to speak, so that there was a place for each of them. There were sleeping bags spread out, four of them, silver, soft, a little bouncy as if they were inflated with air, each resting on a bed of pine needles, which Tess was surprised was amazingly comfortable.

Max was fidgeting, though. That was one of the things he did when he got nervous.

"Breathe," Tess wanted to say to him, but she didn't want to embarrass him in front of Tatiana and Alexei.

Tess was a little jumpy, too. She tried not to shiver, between the "high" left over from performing the aerial ballet stunt, the frightening encounter with Lorenzo, and the almost other-worldly aspect, well, everything that was so difficult to assess. *Where were they?* It took all of Tess's strength to put forth a calm face so that Max wouldn't be frightened.

Alexei seemed to sense, though, both of their discomforts.

"My dad used to tell us a bedtime story," Alexei said. "Sometimes I tell it to Tatiana when we're feeling a little bit alone." Alexei seemed much older than twelve when he said this. Caring, thoughtful, someone who you could rely on if you needed to.

"What happened to your parents?" asked Tess almost without thinking. She added quickly, "I'm sorry, it might be something you don't want to talk about." She realized it might fall into the category of "none of her business."

"No, it's all right," said Alexei. "It is."

He used that phrase the way their dad might have, *It is,*

as if it was something that had happened and there wasn't anything to do about it.

"We had a week off," said Alexei. "I know you think we don't get those, but we do. Usually only four days. We were camped, curiously, in North Devon. It's very beautiful there. Most of it's owned by the National Trust."

Tess looked puzzled. Max explained. "Like parkland, Tess, in America. Yosemite. Yellowstone. Right?"

Alexei nodded. "And our parents went out for a ride in a carriage. It was nighttime. It started to rain. No one's sure what happened. But they were crossing a bridge. No one knows if there was lightning, thunder, or the horse got frightened or slipped or bucked in some way that the carriage landed hard and part of the bridge gave way. They found parts of the carriage . . ." His voice wavered now and Tatiana finished the sentence for him. ". . . but never a trace of them or Lizzie, who was my mother's horse," she said. Tatiana continued, "The water was cold," she said. "No way they would have survived it."

Alexei picked up the story again. "And we stayed here," he said. He started to go on, but Tatiana shook her head. The two of them exchanged a look, and Alexei added simply, "And, we stayed here and kept up the act."

"That's not the way I think of my mother," said

Tatiana, almost interrupting Alexei. "I think of her on the tightrope on pointe, that was always the way she walked on the tightrope, on pointe, doing an arabesque, as if there wasn't any difference between the air and the ground."

"And the way I always think of Dad," said Alexei, "is the first time he let me climb the ladder and clasp the bar and swing. Tara was standing on the ladder below me. I must have been five and Tara pushed me, the way you'd push a kid on a swing, once, twice, maybe it was three times before I had enough speed and motion to let go and tumble through the air and dart straight as an arrow. He was hanging from his knees on a bigger, higher bar, sort of the way we do now, and he caught my hands in his and we went flying through the air together."

Alexei was silent for a moment after that, even the night air was still, the stars above sparkling before he went on.

"But on nights like tonight," he said, trying to sound cheerful, "when we're all a little out of sorts, I always tell Tatiana the story that my father used to tell us. Could I tell it to you now?" he asked Tess and Max.

"I'd like to hear the story," said Tess. "Max?" she asked.

"Sure," he said, trying to sound a bit like a tough guy as he usually thought he was too old for bedtime stories, but this actually sounded like it might be reassuring.

"Okay, then," said Alexei.

"It's a story about a little girl named Anoushka who could touch the sky. That was my dad's pet name for our sister, Anna—Anoushka," he explained.

Tess looked over at Tara, who was sitting a little bit away from them, quietly keeping watch.

Tara was wearing a white shirt that had odd sleeves, largely constructed so they were quite big around her arms, boxy, flowy, almost like they were Japanese.

Tess watched as Tara folded her hands over her head and somehow draped herself in her shirt. She was sitting on the ground, and, like she was doing yoga or something, put her head down on her knees. The way she'd folded her arms, somewhat akimbo, as if she was a dancer draped in the white shirt, made her look, in the crazy night light dusted by the moon, like a white dove with her arms sort of fluttering like wings. She looked so much like a white dove, as if she'd morphed into a white dove, that Tess wondered if she was imagining it. Tara stayed in that position, arms (or wings) fluttering, as Alexei told the bedtime story softly to Tess and Max.

"Once upon a time," Alexei said, "there was a little girl named Anoushka who thought she could touch the sky . . . It wasn't her fault. From the time she was a very little girl her father used to toss her up in the air and catch her, which occasionally made her mother quite nervous, but he was an acrobat and he never tossed her up that high. He also taught her to do somersaults and handstands and cartwheels. Her mother was an acrobat, too, and her mom couldn't help it, she sometimes got the urge to play, too. She taught Anoushka how to dance on a balance beam and sometimes she even let Anoushka's dad toss her up in the air and encourage her to do an in-the-air somersault. Not an easy thing to do, but it turned out Anoushka was very good at it. One day, he threw her up so high that the daylight darkened and she was surrounded by sparkling stars and Anoushka thought she'd actually touched the sky . . ."

That was about all Tess and Max heard, as they were so tired and Alexei's gentle voice was so melodic as he told the story, both of them shut their eyes and fell asleep. And before they knew it, it was morning.

breakfast, carnival-style

There was the smell of fish smoking on the grill.

Tatiana whispered, "We only get a half an hour for breakfast, so we have to hurry. I bet you're hungry."

Tess was. She couldn't remember what she'd eaten yesterday, other than candyfloss.

"What if we just started walking," said Max under his breath, "and made straight for the gate?"

"Definitely not a good idea," said Tatiana, who

immediately took Max's arm. She nodded her head in the direction of one of the tables. Lorenzo was sitting alone watching them. Eyes glued, focused directly on them. He was drinking an espresso from a tiny cup and eating a crunchy cookie called a biscotti.

Max had to admit, attempting an escape while Lorenzo was watching was probably a bad idea.

They took their places in the breakfast line. Each of them picked up a plate and a striped-cloth napkin that looked more like a kitchen towel. The silverware looked like it could use a polish.

"I have to tell you something," Max whispered. "It's sort of odd."

But Lorenzo was looking at them, so Tess whispered back, "You'd better tell me later." Out loud she said, "I'm so glad you slept well," as if that had been the intended subject of their conversation, just in case anyone was listening.

The breakfast line was crowded. Everyone was still not quite dressed up for the carnival. The clown was there. He was wearing overalls instead of a clown suit, but he already had his wig on and white-colored paint on his face.

"Don't worry," he said to Tess, "I never play with balloons until after breakfast." He gave her an impish smile and pulled a white rose out from behind her ear. "Flowers are different," the clown said as he handed it to her. It seemed like he was trying to cheer her up.

The tattooed lady was standing in line right in front of them wearing leggings and a sleeveless T-shirt. She had a tattoo on her right biceps with a picture of a sailing ship with a ripple of water below it and right beneath that on her forearm, a mermaid. It was pretty cool. An eagle on her back with its wings spread out across each of her shoulder blades as if she and the eagle could take off at a moment's notice. She looked at Tess and did a funny dance. And Tess couldn't help it, she felt obliged to return the favor and do a tiny little wiggle, too.

Ben was wearing a white chef's cap. He asked them each to point out exactly which fish they wanted and piled their plates with smoky trout, grilled onions, and baked crispy potatoes that were a little bit burned as he had cooked them right on the coals.

Tess and Max stayed close to Tatiana and Alexei. Tess was struck by the fact that the four of them seemed to be the only children there. Not that they were little children themselves but nonetheless, everyone else seemed to be grown-up.

Alexei led them to a table of their own. Tess ran back

to the buffet table and got an extra glass. She poured some water into it. She placed it in the middle of the table and placed the rose in it. Her mom would appreciate that—that she'd made the effort to make it seem as if everything was normal. There was something normal about a rose in a makeshift vase in the center of the table.

She looked around at the other carnival workers. There was some serious eating going on. Tess wondered how long the workday was for them. *What time did the carnival open? What time did it close? And where, if anywhere, was there an escape route?* She even considered the possibility of tunneling, but that would probably take days of planning, and for all she knew the carnival might pick up stakes and move again before they'd even finished digging the tunnel. *Note to self: abandon the idea of tunneling.*

Tess looked up to see Tara standing with a metal plate stacked with griddle cakes and a bowl of, well, she called it, fresh sage honey.

"I made it this morning," said Tara, implying that she had somehow interacted with a bee-hive, which Tess didn't doubt for a minute. If anyone could tame bees, it might be Tara.

Tess wondered if secretly Tara knew a way to get them home. Or could give her more of a clue of what had to happen before they could go home. But before Tess could ask the question, there was a giant clunk on the table as Lorenzo set his very small coffee cup down with way more force than was needed, causing all the plates and glasses to rattle up and down.

"Your favorite," Tara said to Lorenzo without missing a beat. "Polenta griddle cakes." She placed a small stack on a plate for him.

"Italian cornmeal," said Max.

"What?" said Tess.

"Polenta. Remember. Franny makes polenta with greens and she says it's Italian, so maybe we are in . . ." He stopped as he realized Lorenzo was sitting at the table listening to every word.

"Are where?" asked Tatiana, not understanding why Max had stopped.

"At breakfast," said Tess, brilliantly trying to cover up for him. "My mom's friend Franny makes polenta sometimes for breakfast. But we've never tried it with honey. In fact, I don't think we've ever had homemade honey, at all," said Tess. "Have we, Max?"

"No," said Max. "I never have. This is," he said, giving Tara a very charming smile, the kind he was known for, "very delicious."

After breakfast, when they were walking alone, Tess said to Max, "What did you want to tell me?"

Max looked around to see if anyone else could hear, but they seemed safe at the moment. "When I got up," he said, whispering, "I took a little walk around. I didn't try to go outside of the carnival. I just walked around a bit. Up the hill, I wanted to see if I could see anything . . ."

"And?"

"The pine trees aren't real."

"What do you mean?" asked Tess.

"Well, I don't mean they're not real. They're not planted. They have," he hesitated because this really didn't make any sense, "they have stands on them like Christmas trees. And there are kind of sheets around them. They aren't planted in the ground."

"Maybe they're props," said Tess, trying to be the practical one here. "Maybe they're for a show that we don't know about."

"Maybe," said Max, as if that might make sense. "I just thought it was weird."

"On a scale of one to ten?" asked Tess.

"Okay," said Max, who had to admit this was funny, "on a scale of one to ten, given everything we've been through, I guess you're probably right. It's a three."

"Hopefully the rest of the day might stay that way," said Tess. But even as she said it, she knew that wasn't going to be the case.

As if on cue, Lorenzo appeared out of nowhere and said to Max, "You ready, kid? You're on." And with a nod of his head, directed Max to follow him.

the house of mirrors

Y ou got it, Shorty? Y'just stand here," said Lorenzo.

They were right outside The House of Mirrors, and Lorenzo was again showing Max his spot. "Remember what I told you yesterday," said Lorenzo. "And make sure, if it's a group, they go in together. If someone's in line by themselves, you send a couple folks right in after them. People get a lot less scared when they're not alone."

Lorenzo had directed Max to follow him right after

breakfast and stationed him at the entrance to The House of Mirrors. Max still wondered what would happen if he made for the front gate. Just took off on a sprint. Was this one of those times when it would be better for Tess if he tried to escape without her and went to get help? They obviously needed some help. The only thing he was frightened about was what might be outside the gates. *Where were they? Was there an outside?* That probably seemed silly, but Max had been through something like this before.

He kept turning the events over in his mind, and the only thing he could come up with was that the carnival had run away with them. And he couldn't lose the thought that it was sort of his fault. If only he hadn't played with the levers and the pulleys and that thing that looked like a steering wheel.

Max figured he might make it to the gate. But the thing he was worried about was, if he made it outside, would he be able to find his way back in again?

Lorenzo was talking to him, a blue streak, and leading him through The House of Mirrors. He was showing Max the secret escape exit.

Halfway into The House of Mirrors, make a right, then a left at the next pane of glass, then a right, almost as if you were going in a circle. And . . . there was a blank pane. No one would ever notice it. A blank pane, that led straight out into the carnival again.

Max realized he was uniquely suited for this job. He was very good at math. He had counted the steps they'd taken on the first pathway through the mirror, 14 steps, then the right turn; 12 steps, then the left turn; 10 steps, and then a right again, 8 steps. 44 steps in all.

He made up a memory trick: double fours.

That was how he was going to remember 44.

14, 12, 10, 8; 14, 12, 10, 8. Max repeated the number of steps over in his mind. And he realized there was a second memory trick, deduct 2 from each: 14, 12, 10, 8.

He was wearing the carnival uniform again, drab gray, almost the color of an elephant's skin. It was a jumpsuit that had old-fashioned tortoiseshell buttons. Max figured they were really made out of plastic, not tortoiseshell. As to how he had come to be wearing the uniform, as he didn't remember putting it on in the morning . . . ? He distinctly remembered putting on his jeans, which had been by his sleeping bag in the morning. But now he wasn't sure of that, either. He was definitely wearing the carnival uniform now. He figured if he asked Tara how he came to be wearing it, she probably would have answered, "Carnival Magic." And frankly, he couldn't come up with a better explanation.

sky dancing

The poster had been changed overnight.

THE BREATHTAKING
BARANOVAS

starring

Tatiana, Alexei, and introducing Tessa

That's what it said. He'd changed her name even.
Added an *a* at the end.

And there was her picture painted where Tatiana and Alexei's sister Anna had been the day before.

Tess wondered who could have painted it. It was a startling likeness of her. Her hair in an updo, like the one Tara had fashioned for her the day before, and wearing the costume she'd had on with the silver stars sewn onto it.

Tess wondered if someone had taken a photograph and used it as a model and painted it last night.

Wasn't Lorenzo supposed to ask her if this was what she wanted to do?

She looked down. She was still wearing the jeans she'd put on that morning.

But instead of her T-shirt, she was now wearing the leotard with the silver stars sewn onto it—the leotard she was wearing in the poster.

Was it like a magic mirror or something? If she looked at it long enough was the rest of her outfit going to transform, and would her hair suddenly turn into an updo? And she would be a carnival worker? Sort of the way Max was wearing the carnival worker's uniform at breakfast, even though that wasn't what he'd put on, at all. She was suddenly very frightened. And somehow she couldn't pull her glance away from her image on the poster. She shut her eyes. She put her hands over her eyes so that she couldn't see it.

When she opened her eyes, there was already a line for tickets to the show, a long line. The carnival was open.

Tess darted as quickly as she could into the blue tent before Lorenzo could see her or someone else could find her or catch her, but she wasn't sure where she could hide.

She ran backstage instinctively, to where the dressing room was, hoping she would find Tatiana or even Tara. But there was no one there. She wondered where Tatiana was and how much time there was before the show actually was scheduled to begin.

She heard footsteps in the tent, someone with a long stride walking.

"Tess-a." His voice was sort of sing-song. "Tess-a," he said again. "I know you're in here." That faint Italian accent that was so recognizable. "You cannot hide from me," he said, frightening her all the more. "Tess-a . . ." The *can not* was almost like two words, which made it all the more menacing.

She felt a hand on her arm. Tess turned around defiantly, prepared to face her opponent with no fear at all. She was enormously relieved to see it was Alexei.

"I can't do it," Tess said to Alexei.

Tess didn't usually question her ability to do anything.

But in this case, she knew her own limitations. It was just too risky. She was not an expert in aerial ballet!

"I'm not trained the way you are," she said. "What if I was to fall again?"

"I know," he said, "and Lorenzo doesn't have the right to ask you or force you. But we have to hurry. We have to figure out how to get you away . . . before it's too late for you to get away."

Tess wasn't sure what he meant by this. But she had a feeling Alexei knew that at some point she and Max might never be able to leave. She pushed that thought away. Whatever they had to do, they would do it. There was no way she wasn't going to see her parents again. Or Aunt Evie. She and Max would figure out a way to get away. She was certain of it. She also knew she had to get as far away as possible from the aerial ballet trapeze before she was forced (or compelled) to perform again.

"Tess-a." They heard Lorenzo calling her. He sounded as if he was very near. "Tess-a. Don't think that you can get a-way . . ."

"Shh." Alexei put his finger to his mouth and took her hand. He guided her through the backstage, a labyrinthian obstacle course that he knew by heart, avoiding strange doorframes that led to nowhere but were used onstage as props by a magician; large tubs from years ago, when they had dancing seals; elaborate scaffolding for acrobatic acts and for the tech guys, none of whom seemed to be on-site, to run the backstage wires, and spotlights, and special effects for the shows. Hammers, oversized screwdrivers, and nails littered the floor, and there were at least four ladders that a person could have run into and knocked over, making an enormous amount of noise . . . But Alexei led her silently and brilliantly to the very back of the tent.

He put his index finger up again, the way he'd done the first time he'd let them in, and as if it was a magic X-acto knife, made a slit down the silk and revealed, for a moment, a door, a curtain, that he held open for her.

They could still hear Lorenzo calling her name: "Tess-a Tess-a."

"You go ahead," he said. "I'll stay here and try to distract him. You have to try to get away. Tell Max you have to try to get away. And I'll find you. I promise," he said.

"No," said Tess. "I promise, I'll find you."

Tess wondered if he knew how much she hoped that would be true. And how frightened she was that it might not be.

Alexei held her hand tightly for a moment as if he really didn't want to let her go. And then pushed her, right out the silk curtain, onto the grounds of the carnival.

She heard that funny zipper-like sound again as the blue tent closed up behind her.

inside the house of mirrors

I don't have time to explain, Max," said Tess. She was almost out of breath, as she'd run so quickly to find her brother at the entrance to The House of Mirrors.

"We have to get out of here now."

"Get out of here?" said Max. "You said we couldn't leave."

"He's trying to make me be one of the Baranovas. He wants me to replace Anna. He's changed the poster overnight. And now I'm there instead of Anna. My face on the poster. I'm not risking my neck to do aerial ballet. And look . . ." She gestured to the leotard she had on. Her jeans were still over it. "I didn't put it on this morning. I put on a T-shirt. And now . . ." She gestured to the leotard again. "And he keeps calling my name. Well, not *my* name. He's changed my name to Tessa."

Tess didn't have to explain who "he" was. Max knew she was referring to Lorenzo.

"We have to leave. Now, Max. I'm afraid if we don't, we'll never be able to. I'm afraid that I might . . ."

She didn't have to finish that sentence.

"Alexei said we couldn't leave last night, when the carnival was closed. But now he's telling me we have to escape, as if somehow if we don't, we may never be able to leave. I mean, what if the carnival moves again . . ." She didn't have to finish that sentence, either.

"Let's think logically," said Max.

"There isn't time," said Tess.

"Sometimes if you take a beat, you save time," said Max, sounding wiser than his years. "Take a deep breath. I think you might be right—I don't think we can walk out of the gate. We don't know what's out there or if we could get back in. I'm not even sure we could make it to the gate

without one of them finding us. Lorenzo's sidekick Izzy."
He shivered at the thought of getting caught.

And then Max had an idea. What if they used the secret
exit that Lorenzo had shown him and ducked out that way?
Maybe. Just maybe that would work. At least they'd be trying
a back way, not quite out in front of The House of Mirrors,
but out the back door, when they might be able to blend in
with the carnival-goers and make an escape—*escape where*,
Max wasn't sure—but escape was sounding promising.

He took her hand. "It's okay," he said, acting so much
like her big brother instead of her little one that Tess was
ashamed that she'd panicked. It wasn't like her. But then
again, it had totally freaked her out to see her face, her
image, on the poster.

"Right this moment," said Max, "we have to find
somewhere to hide. Shh," he said, and he meant it.

They could hear Lorenzo in the distance, through the
noise of the carnival, calling her name. Her new name.
"Tess-a . . . Tess-a."

Max led Tess quickly into The House of Mirrors,
which it occurred to Tess was a completely ridiculous place
to hide, as everywhere she turned she saw her reflection
and Max's and assumed anyone else could see them, too.

She also thought she heard the beginning of footsteps

running after them, and turning back didn't seem to be an option.

"It's okay," said Max, pulling her hand, compelling her to follow him even farther into The House of Mirrors. "Down one corridor. Take a left. Another corridor, take a right." As if he knew it like the back of his hand.

"I might have a plan," Max whispered. "I think I have a plan."

Max's plan was to run to the secret exit, although he realized Lorenzo knew where that was, too. But he had to try it. He needed more time to think. He followed the pattern he'd memorized: double fours. 44 steps in all. 14, then 12, then 10, then 8 . . .

But before they reached the secret exit, Max saw it out of the corner of his eye . . . He saw it. Exactly what Lorenzo had described.

He grabbed Tess's arm to get her to stop, too.

There it was. There was the image of another carnival. Directly at the spot where sometimes people screamed as they looked into the mirror, mesmerized, as if they couldn't help themselves from looking. It was almost ghostly, and the pane of glass didn't have their reflection in it, at all. It seemed to be a porthole, a view, to another carnival on the other side of the glass.

Max was still holding Tess's hand. He had to be careful not to lose her in The House of Mirrors. A wrong turn and—he couldn't imagine what it would be like if he lost Tess.

He put his finger up in another gesture of "shh."

They could hear harsh footsteps, from all directions, Lorenzo running after them, his voice calling, "Tess-a Tess-a." There was more than one set of footsteps. As if Lorenzo had enlisted help. And they seemed to be coming directly to them from all sides. Lorenzo knew where the secret exit was, too. *What if they were trapped?*

Max pointed to the mirror.

The image was clear, well, not completely clear, as the color was sort of monotone. But it was as if there *was* another carnival there, just on the other side of the glass. *Or was it a reflection?*

Max turned around to try to see if that could possibly be true. Could the mirrors reflect that way, one off the other, off the other, off the other, so that what they were really seeing was a reflection of the carnival outside?

No, it wasn't true. It was an image of another carnival, an old-fashioned version in some ways, the women wearing long skirts, with fancy buttoned blouses, and hairstyles from another time. The little boys were wearing shorts and short-sleeved button-down shirts, not T-shirts. The men were wearing old-fashioned suits, no ties.

"No one's wearing sneakers," said Max, as if that one sentence summed it up.

A clown passed by on the other side of the glass.

He wasn't a bit like the nice clown who'd given Tess a rose earlier that morning. This clown was as white as a mummy, with theatrical black brows, and dark black eye-liner, and the scariest frown, also in black, painted around his lips. He turned his face toward them for a minute and opened his mouth wide in an almost terrifying smile, if a smile could be meant to be terrifying.

The footsteps were getting closer.

They heard Lorenzo call out loudly, "Tess-a . . ."

The word reverberated through The House of Mirrors. It was as if the sound was reflected off every pane of glass, echoing itself, "Tess-a, Tess-a, Tess-a, Tess-a, Tess-a." The echoed sound of the word started almost before the first one stopped, so that the words, the syllables, doubled on themselves, the second "Tess" starting before the first "a" had even been pronounced, which somehow made it even more frightening, as if there was a symphony of Lorenzos after them. Or a frightening number of people calling Tess's new name. Tess-a, Tess-a, Tess-a. *Was there one set of footsteps or three or were there more?* It was as if the footsteps, too, seemed to echo, bounce, reverberate off the panes of glass, and it was almost impossible to tell where they were coming from.

The clown was staring them down again from the other side of the glass. A scary theatrical work of art, he was, almost demonic as he stared directly at Tess and Max. Tess screamed, which Max anticipated, and he put his hand over her mouth to stop her scream. But it started to echo, too, bouncing off the mirrors, so that even though she stopped screaming, the scream continued on and caused her to understandably scream again.

The clock started to tick. The telltale sign, as the seconds on the seven-minute clock started to wind down.

Max wondered what happened when it got to seven. Lorenzo had never told him that.

The footsteps sounded lighter now, steady, intent, tiptoe-y, coming closer and closer. Tess felt someone touch her arm. She screamed again and turned to see him . . . and was relieved that it was Alexei.

"I thought you might need some help," said Alexei to Max, completely ignoring Tess in this moment.

Tess tried to calm herself. She stuck her hands into her pockets and took a deep breath. As her left hand touched the needle, it was almost like an electric current, a tiny jolt to her hand. There was a bright glint of light. Tess pulled the needle out of her pocket and held it up. It was as if it was quietly vibrating.

Both Max and Alexei stepped away from her, as if they were giving her space or were somewhat surprised at what was occurring.

There was a sharp piercing sound, a crazy cracking could be heard, as the mirror started to shatter. So loudly anyone could hear it, a sure clue to their whereabouts, was the sound of the glass breaking. Then there was another burst of light that seemed to be coming from the mirror itself. Max, Alexei, and Tess just stared as the mirror seemed to get brighter and brighter.

Tess held the needle up to it, and a halo of light, all the colors of the rainbow, seemed to be reflected in the one pane of glass as it broke into pieces and reformed, the way a kaleidoscope geometrically reshapes, red, yellow, blue, purple. In triangles and flower-like patterns, in the center of which a round hole appeared with a clear view of what really seemed to be a carnival on the other side of the mirror.

Alexei nodded to both of them and put his index finger through the hole, and as he did, it widened. The other footsteps were accompanied by voices now. "This way. I hear them this way," they heard someone say,

"Tess-a," the unmistakable sound of Lorenzo calling her.

Alexei said, "There isn't any other choice." He pushed his arm in farther, and the space became almost big enough to step through. And held his arm there as if it was a way to hold a door open. "I'll see you again, I promise," said Alexei. And then he added the strangest thing, "After you touch the sky."

Tess shut her eyes for a moment. When she opened them Alexei was still staring at her, and for a moment, she stared back. She didn't cry. It wasn't in Tess's nature to cry.

"Go ahead, Max," she said. "I'll be right behind you."

Max stepped through. Tess stepped through the glass after him, still holding on to Alexei's hand as if she needed to balance or have something to hold on to.

She pulled her hand back. Let go. From opposite sides, Tess and Alexei locked eyes in a look of determination and friendship, tinged a little bit with sadness, as the colored panes of glass faded and turned to the brightest silver. As the pane reformed back into a flawless mirror, the clock stopped ticking. All sight of Alexei disappeared. And she and Max were all alone now and definitely on the other side, wherever in the world *that* was.

the other side

They were out in an open field. That was what it seemed like at first. It was quite crowded with people in somewhat old-fashioned dress. The women were all wearing long skirts, at least below the knee. The little kids were dressed in, well, Tess, didn't know quite *how* to describe it, baggy trousers, peasant dresses, short pants that didn't really resemble shorts.

There was a tent in the distance. Something that

looked like a Ferris wheel. They were somehow at the edge of the carnival standing in an open field. Well, it wasn't exactly an open field.

It was a big dirt pad, definitely man-made, almost circular. All the greenery and rocks had been pulled or smoothed out of it. Around the perimeter, there were large patches of olive trees giving some shade from the hot afternoon sun.

Tess knew they were olives, as Aunt Evie had two in her orchard in Hampshire next to the fig tree, which she said she'd brought home as a souvenir from a trip she'd taken with Uncle John to Greece. Lots of people in England had done that, imported plants and tropicals. Tess had even seen some palms at the Paignton ZOO. Aunt Evie had promised that one day they would cure their own olives, marinate them in olive oil, garlic, and herbs. Max always thought it was funny that the word you used to pickle olives was *cure*, as if there was something wrong with them to begin with. This whole train of thought was making Tess homesick—well, more than homesick—she wondered when she would see Aunt Evie again and wished that they were at the zoo.

Tess realized she was the only *girl* wearing jeans. Max's weird carnival uniform kind of fit in. What worried

Tess most was the footwear. Lace-up boots. And nobody, nobody except her was wearing sneakers. A little girl was watching them.

"Remember that school trip I took, Max," said Tess, "to Williamsburg, Virginia? All the people were wearing Colonial outfits. And they performed historical plays. Maybe this is like that," she said, trying to make sense of it and calm Max at the same time. "Maybe at this carnival, they dress up in old-fashioned dress. Mom told us about that Renaissance Faire she went to in L.A. once. Remember?"

But Max wasn't really paying attention to Tess any more. The sound above them was familiar and not, at the same time. It wasn't a helicopter. But something was definitely going on in the sky.

Everyone in the crowd was looking upward. As the noise came closer . . . and closer . . . and closer. Until they streaked over head.

Four old-fashioned biplanes making loops in the sky. Circling each other, dovetailing, flying in a straight line, and then forming a perfect square. The red plane executed a steep dive directly toward the ground and pulled out of it twenty-five feet above the crowd to cheers and waves. The yellow plane hovered directly over for a moment, and then someone jumped out. That scary moment before the parachute opened. The pilot glided dramatically down to the ground, carrying something that when he got nearer was revealed to be a green flag with a red dinosaur on it and a white sky.

Tess looked at Max questioningly.

Well, maybe it wasn't a dinosaur. Maybe it was a dragon. What country could that be?

Max shook his head. He tried to remember if there was a soccer team that displayed that flag.

Before Tess or Max could say anything more, there were "oohs" and "ahhs" from the crowd and various people pointing, as a man in what appeared to be a similar jumpsuit to Max's with an aviator helmet on his head performed a spectacular wing walk on the black plane and then totally wowed the crowd by hanging from his hands. He then performed an amazing somersault up into the air, somehow staying in league with the forward motion of the plane. He must have been attached somehow, that was the only possible explanation. He landed perfectly on his feet again on the top wing. It was stunning. No one in the crowd could breathe until he exited back into the plane, which remarkably he seemed to be piloting.

"Can a biplane fly by itself, Max?"

"Umm, when car engines get old they replace them," Max said as if he was considering this theory himself. "It's an old plane. That makes sense. It must have a modern engine and he put it on autopilot. I don't know, though. Maybe old-fashioned biplanes have an automatic setting, too."

"Oh," said Tess because that sort of made sense.

Tess noticed that all the other kids at the carnival seemed to be accompanied by adults. Tess put her chin down and said to Max under her breath, "I think we have to say we work here, if anyone asks us. It seems like we're the only kids without parents or a grown-up here."

"Okay, but," said Max, ever practical as always, "what if the person who asks us works here?"

"That could be a problem," Tess muttered back to him.

The little girl was still staring at them. Tess smiled, as if that might disarm her. But instead it encouraged her, and she pulled her mother's arm and pointed in Tess's direction.

Tess grabbed Max's hand and darted into the center of the crowd. "Stay close to me, Max. We're short," she said. "It'll be easy to hide in plain sight."

This sort of did make sense since everyone except that

little girl was watching the dramatic show in the air and no one was paying much attention to any strangers next to them, especially not to two kids who seemed to be sticking close to one another and enjoying the show, too.

The planes flew back into formation again, one, two, three, four, right in line with each other, like forward march, and then the red plane pulled out and up ahead, then the blue plane flew in right behind it, then the yellow, and then the black plane at the back, so they were in a straight line. They flew that way almost in a semicircle, then made an approach for the runway, which Tess realized was directly in front of the crowd.

a very dramatic landing

The red plane landed first to shouts and cheers, and slowed to a stop at the very end of the runway. Then the blue plane landed and also hit the brakes and stopped behind the red plane. Then the yellow one did the same. And then the black plane landed, seeming almost to set off multicolored sparks as its wheels hit the ground, not frightening, almost like rainbow bursts. Tess realized she had put her hands in her pockets, and she was holding on to the needle. She wondered if she was causing the streaks of light. Tess let go as the black plane came to a complete stop directly behind the other three.

Drums, a trombone, the big metal clang of cymbals, or tin pans banging together, Tess wasn't sure which as she couldn't see the orchestra, if there was an orchestra. Then she saw it was a marching band, in blue, white, and red costumes, coming out to celebrate the stars of the show—the amazing aviators who had each just successfully landed their plane.

"Attention." The bandleader had an accent that Tess couldn't quite place. On command, the marching band came to a stop, but each continued to march, legs up, legs down, exactly in place without the accompaniment of their musical instruments. The door of the red plane opened, and the pilot debarked. Next, the blue plane, and that pilot stepped out of the cockpit and onto the ground. Next, the yellow one, whose pilot did the same, bowing gracefully after he'd descended. And then with a slight flourish, almost a skip in the air, the pilot of the black plane landed and put his hand on his hip, in a casual attitude and acknowledgement of his extreme achievement.

Tess had now linked her pinkie in to Max's. "If we

hold hands," she'd said, "someone might think that we're really little kids and that we're lost."

Max was mesmerized by the pilots, and he led Tess, inadvertently since their pinkies were linked and she had to follow him, effortlessly through the crowd, until they were almost up at the front with a clear view of the pilots on the runway.

There was a drum roll, as if something amazing was about to happen.

With another flourish, the pilots, in unison, each unsnapped their helmets and triumphantly removed them, holding the helmet in front of them almost as if it was a medal of sorts. At least, three of them did. The pilot of the black plane waited, a long beat. Another drum roll. And then the fourth pilot unsnapped the helmet, shook "his" head, and it was revealed, as the pilot's hair brilliantly cascaded down below her shoulders, in dark waves and curls, that despite the jumpsuit and the amazing athletic wing-walk display, including the exhibition of truly remarkable arm strength, that the wing walker was really a woman.

A giant round of applause, hurrahs, and yelps from the crowd for the three male pilots and the very beautiful female pilot who looked as if she might be eighteen. If she was even that old. Tess couldn't tell. But Tess was impressed that the young woman hadn't made (or been asked to make) any silly concessions (like wearing a swimsuit) and was just dressed exactly the same as the rest of the crew. Absolutely no question, though, that she was the star.

A line had formed immediately. Well, four lines. Four straight lines. People were holding autograph books and pieces of paper with pens. The longest line, by far, was for her.

The music started again, but it was more the way a nursery rhyme would sound or a music box or a carousel. La La La la la la la La La La la la la la There was the sound of a very light cymbal, too, and bells, a lot like a carousel.

Tess felt her pinkie being pulled again. She looked at Max, who was staring at the female pilot, a little starstruck himself, and slinking them in almost to the front of the line that had formed to see her. Luckily nobody called them on it. Tess was very careful to look down. *Don't engage.* That was something her dad had taught her, about a way not to get into an argument with someone on the playground, not that he'd anticipated an instance like this. But it seemed to apply. *Don't engage. That way no one will engage with you.*

La La La   la la la la   La La La   la la la la . . .

It was hard not to want to dance to it. What kind of music was that?

Tess noticed she could see painted horses on a carousel and poles, and a pointed, painted canopy top of the tent off in the distance. Was it a large blue tent? But everything looked paler somehow. It made sense about the biplanes, that the yellow and red would have become fainter from all those years flying around in the sun. But everything was like that. Even the clothes the people around her were wearing seemed faded, as if they'd been washed too many times. But that didn't explain why everyone was so pale. She wondered if she and Max looked pale, too, if there was something about the light or there was a cloud cover blocking the sun. But the sky was clear, just a paler blue than she'd ever seen a sky before.

the autograph

There was a little boy next to Tess who was eating a candyfloss.

That was reassuring. Except the candyfloss was white. Maybe it was organic. She'd never seen white candyfloss before, only pink or blue.

They were almost first in line now. There was a gracefulness to the female pilot that Tess noticed immediately, as if she had the aspect of a dancer.

Max convinced the kid with the candyfloss to rip a piece of paper out of the notebook the kid was carrying so that Max *could* get an autograph. Tess stood by anxiously while Max negotiated for the paper.

"You wouldn't let me borrow a piece of paper, would you?" Max asked the kid, although *borrow* wasn't exactly what he meant.

The kid was really nice and just said, "Ie, Ie!" He tore a piece out carefully and gave it to Max. "Isn't she amazing? Why me and my family come." His English was funny, as if it wasn't his first language. "Ie, Ie," almost as if it was two syllables. What language was that? It didn't sound like English exactly; maybe it was Italian. But then Max realized that wasn't a sign of anything, as it was summer and the kid and his parents could just be vacationing tourists.

Then Max and Tess were first in line.

Tess was mesmerized by the female pilot, too. She was just as pale as everyone else at the carnival, but her skin was flawless, as flawless as if she was a porcelain doll. She had long dark lashes and eyes that were almost brown or green. Aunt Evie would probably say they were hazel. But what fascinated Tess most were her hands and how extraordinarily strong they looked. She wasn't very tall, but her hands were both pretty and agile and looked so powerful that the fountain pen she was holding seemed almost like a toy. "To both of you?" she asked.

"No," said Tess, "just sign it to my brother, Max." Tess thought it should be something that was just to him.

"Max," said Max, "Max Barnes," reaching his hand out to shake hers. It was important to him that she knew he was polite. "And this is my sister, Tess."

"Okay, Max Barnes," she said. She took his hand for a moment and nodded to him.

"Max Barnes," she repeated as she wrote his name. And then she scrawled something underneath and below that signed her own name, in very clear but decorative handwriting. Tess didn't know what she wrote as she was on the other side of the table, so the writing was upside down.

"Thanks," said Max, taking the paper from her and holding it as if it were a precious stone.

a very valuable signature

As they were walking away, Tess said, "Let me see the paper."

Max hesitated. He didn't even want to share the paper with her.

"I promise I'm not going to crumple it," said Tess.

He handed her the autograph very carefully, accompanied by a look that suggested she should be very very careful with it herself.

Tess couldn't believe what she saw. She couldn't believe what the pilot had written. Was it possible? The paper read:

Max Barnes,

Touch the sky!!!

Anna Baranova

"Max. Max. Max." Max was walking ahead of her. "Max, stop. Max, did you look at this?"

She carefully handed him back the personalized signed paper. That was what Alexei had said to her when he'd first, somewhat magically, let her into the blue tent. *Touch the sky.*

Of course, she should have known immediately. Tess had seen her picture on the poster. At least, it had been her image on the poster until someone had replaced it with the image of Tess.

Anna looked a little older than she had in the poster on the tent at the carnival. But Tess should have recognized her. She looked a lot like Tatiana.

Anna Baranova. Alexei and Tatiana's older sister.

Max looked at the autograph and he realized it, too. *Anna Baranova.* They'd found her.

The realization of who she was raised so many other questions that Tess's head was spinning.

That little girl was looking at her again. Pulling her mother's hand and pointing at Tess. Tess ducked behind a family of six that was walking past and pulled Max with her.

Tess realized that she hadn't had anything to eat since breakfast. The sun was beating down intensely.

"I have a headache," Tess said to Max. Suddenly she felt unsteady on her feet.

Max guided her, following the funny family of six, over to the grove of olive trees. He reasoned Tess might feel better out of the sun, assuming she didn't faint first. She was walking strangely, as if she *was* about to topple over. He pinched her arm. Tess winced.

"Sorry," said Max. "I didn't mean to hurt you, Tess. I was frightened you *might* faint and then someone would come help us and then . . . Did you know you get a shot of adrenaline when you get hurt? It happens organically."

"No," said Tess, "I didn't know that, but thanks, actually. I needed a wake-up call."

She looked behind her to see if the little girl was still watching her, but thankfully she was nowhere in sight.

There were four wooden picnic tables underneath the olive trees. The family of six had sat down at one of them. On another, was almost a buffet-style banquet. There were small glasses, just the right size for juice, that seemed to have alternately pale orange and pale yellow, maybe it was lemon or orange-flavored, liquid in them. *Juice? Soda? It was hard to tell.* It looked as if they were free for the taking unless they belonged to a family. Max figured he still had some money left if they were for sale. There were so many glasses, it looked as if they were there for the folks who'd gone to the show.

Max picked up one that was filled with orange liquid and took a sip, protectively tasting it to make sure it seemed okay to give it to Tess. It tasted like fresh orange juice with bubbly water in it, not quite as sweet as soda. "It's pretty good. Here, Tess," he said, handing it to her, "I think you'll feel better if you drink it.

"And look," he said, "this looks like a regular old cheese sandwich, even though it's on fancy bread. Well, the cheese is kind of pale. But didn't we have white cheddar in England?" *Maybe they were still in England, after all.* He took a bite as if he was testing it, too. He nodded and handed it to her. And then he took one for himself.

They sat down under one of the olive trees and Tess

drank an entire orange juice, which had an instant effect. It was almost like she could think again. Although, there were so many things to think about, including the family that was sitting at the table next to them.

"They look like a normal family, don't they, Max?"

Max looked at her questioningly.

"I mean they all have red hair. Sort of. It's not quite red, it's more auburn."

What she really wanted to say was faded red, but she didn't know how to say that. "And they're all really pale, aren't they? But then again redheaded folks are sometimes pale. But look at the juice. It's not quite orange, is it? I mean, it's not as bright as orange juice."

"It's not as bright as the orange juice we have in the United States."

"Maybe it's paler in England. What was that flag? Are we in a different country?" She nodded toward the redheaded family. "What language are they speaking?"

Max leaned in. It didn't sound like a language he knew. Was it Polish? He didn't know. He'd never been to Poland. Or met anyone from Poland that he remembered. Was it Russian? His dad had a couple of Russian friends. Maybe. That might be what it was.

The clown walked by, dressed all in white. He was

wearing white makeup with that oversized frown in black lipstick painted around his mouth instead of a smile. He had black tears painted on his cheeks just below his eyes. And he didn't make any attempt to perform for any of the kids. It was almost like he was a scary mime. Tess wasn't liking the look of this.

She could see the autograph lines had thinned, and there were only a few folks left.

They had to talk to Anna. Anna might understand. At least, Tess thought that Anna might, if they were able to explain it, that is. If . . . and if she really was who they thought . . .

Max had the same thought almost at the same time. They stood up in unison. Sometimes they did have almost psychic communication. They instinctively held pinkies again. Tess whispered, "We have to look like we belong here. Don't look frightened. Don't look around. Keep your eyes down, Max."

They were halfway across the field now. They saw someone vaguely familiar. It looked like Lorenzo, the carnival owner, except this gentleman was older, with gray hair and a long, wispy gray-white beard. He, too, was walking toward Anna.

"Chase me, Max," said Tess not waiting for him but

quickly breaking into a run. She knew that if they pretended to be kids playing, no one would think that it was strange. Max took her cue.

She let him catch up to her just as they reached Anna, and Tess laughed, the way a little kid would laugh when her brother was chasing her. She turned around and tickled him in the side so he started laughing, too.

The older gentleman was standing next to Anna now as if he were her coach or her owner or, Tess hated to think, her guard. Tess realized he probably was the carnival owner. There was something so overprotective and strange about the way he stood beside her. But Tess noticed Anna didn't look the least bit frightened. Of course not. Anna was a Baranova, and she could wing walk, she probably wasn't afraid of anything.

Tess remembered what Alexei had said to her. *Touch the sky.*

"I'm sorry," said Tess, as if she was a fan. "I'm not meaning to bother you. You look so familiar. I know . . . I know you're, I mean, well-known, well, famous, but you look like someone I've met before."

"That's not possible," the older gentleman answered for her. "We've never been in this part of Wales before."

Wales? Is that where they were? Tess wished she could

remember her geography better. *Wasn't that a little country north of England?*

Tess hit Max slightly with her elbow in his side and hoped he understood what she was asking. (Sometimes people kick someone under the table to quietly suggest to them they should be quiet—but in this case Tess was trying to signal Max to start to talk.) Max got the message. And began to talk up a blue streak.

Max looked directly at the gentleman. "Was that Welsh those people were speaking?" he asked. "That's so interesting."

The older man had the strangest voice, almost as if it was coming out of a megaphone. "People come from all over," he said, "to visit Alberto's Carnival Extravaganza. I'm Alberto," he said, "in case you didn't figure that out yet."

"No," said Max, "I'd figured that out. The biplane show is amazing!"

Tess leaned into Anna and whispered, "I'm Tess. I think I know your sister."

Anna stood up straight and put her shoulders back. "That's not possible," she said, but thankfully she whispered, too.

"I thought you might say that," Tess answered softly.

185

"What are you two talking about?" Alberto blasted at her.

"Oh, nothing, really," said Tess. "I think—I think she's extraordinary. Her performance was astonishing. I was just telling her how much I'd always wanted to touch the sky." Tess knew the phrase would ring true to Anna. It's what she'd written on the paper. It's what Alexei had said to her. "And I was just going to ask how old Anoushka was when she first knew that she wanted to fly."

Tess could see the instant understanding in Anna's eyes. *"Anoushka."* Nobody knew she was called that except her family. But her reaction was completely unexpected.

"No one calls me that except my family, and that was a long time ago. Sometimes fans know too much about you." Anna became instantly distant and pulled herself up as if she was about to leave. But then she noticed something about Tess.

"You're wearing the leotard," she said.

Tess nodded.

"What leotard??!" the older man chimed in, practically shaking the table he was speaking so loudly.

"Don't you remember?" asked Anna. She was lying now, too. Thinking as fast as she could. "One year Lorenzo made leotards and sold them to the kids who came to the

186

show. She has one on. I haven't seen one for years . . . See the silver sparkly star? They're real fans. I think they're funny, Alberto," Anna announced emphatically. It was obvious from what Anna had just said that he knew Lorenzo. Max noted that Alberto was an Italian name, too, and wondered if the man was related to Lorenzo.

"The two kids?" Alberto said, pointing to them. "Funny?!!"

"Can't I bring them to the trailer? Just for a little. Julian won't mind. He always likes company. This is Alberto," she introduced them. "Max, Tess."

Alberto barely nodded.

Anna changed the tone of her voice, softer now but with an edge. "You know it always takes me a little bit of time, Alberto, to wind down after I've done an air show, and it might be fun to have a couple of kids around for a second who have a lot of energy and excitement. Julian's my guardian," she explained to Tess and Max. "And I'm sure he's already started dinner. Are *your* parents here?" Anna asked them.

"No, they dropped us," said Tess, which wasn't really true at all. Aunt Evie had dropped them. But *where* exactly she'd dropped them and *how long ago* that was, was a question that was up for grabs.

"And, for sure, they won't be back for hours," Max added. It did worry him and Tess felt the same, that Aunt Evie had probably returned to the carnival, or at least the site of the carnival where she'd dropped them, and by now she might be nearly hysterical.

Alberto still hadn't agreed.

Then Anna said, with an ever softer edge to her voice, "You want Anna to perform tomorrow, don't you, Alberto?" She asked it tauntingly, referring to herself in the third person. "Well, then, Anna wants Tess and Max to have dinner with her tonight."

Alberto immediately nodded.

"That's settled, then," said Anna, and she took off.

"Come on," she said to Tess and Max, who were a little surprised at this performance but quickly and willingly followed her before Alberto could say another word.

Anna whispered to Tess and Max, as they were walking away, "Don't think badly of me. Sometimes I have to act like a 'star,' throw a little fit, in order to get him to do what I want. I don't normally refer to myself as 'Anna.' I don't want you to think I'm full of myself in that way. It's been hard. Trying on me. I have to keep my wits about me all the time. If they had their way, they'd keep me totally locked up." She didn't explain who "they" were.

"Come on, then." Anna was walking so fast, taking extra big strides, that it was difficult to keep step with her. "Quick," said Anna, to Tess and Max. "We don't want anyone to see us. Are you sure your parents won't be coming back for you soon?"

"That's one of the things we wanted to talk to you about," said Tess.

the traveller's wagon

They followed Anna across the dirt pad and onto a wild grassy field. They turned down a road that ran through even more familiar deep, green grassy fields dotted with white and purple flowers. There was a trailer parked ahead that also looked oddly familiar. Strangely, it did look a lot like what Aunt Evie had called the traveller's wagon they'd seen parked by the side of the road in Devon. Remarkably like it. It was elaborately painted, carved from wood, with yellow wooden somewhat mismatched wheels, the front wheels were smaller than the back ones. It was beautiful, very ornately crafted and painted, with gold and green curlicues that edged the roof.

Standing freely next to it, not tethered or roped in any way, unsaddled, was an exquisite black mare whose illustrious pedigree Tess could only imagine. Drop-dead gorgeous, if a horse can be drop-dead gorgeous. She was a very large horse but quite lively for her size, delicate, graceful, and there was an antic look in the horse's eye as if she recognized Tess immediately as a kindred spirit.

Max's eye was caught by the traveller's car. "It looks like the wagon we saw yesterday," said Max. "Doesn't it, Tess? Well," he added, "it looks newer somehow. But it's kind of the same model."

"The same as *what*?" asked Anna, who hadn't quite heard what Max had said.

Tess repeated Max almost exactly. "It looks like a wagon we saw yesterday," Tess explained. "I think it was yesterday. Maybe the day before? In Devon," she added.

"Is that where they are?" asked Anna. "Devon? Is that where Alexei and Tatiana are? Devon-by-the-Sea?"

Neither Max nor Tess knew exactly how to answer that question.

"Well," said Tess, choosing her words carefully, "that's where we first met them."

Anna didn't pursue this line of questioning, at first. Instead she said, very excitedly, "Tell me how they are," smiling when she said it. "Tell me anything you can. Are they okay?"

"Spectacular," said Tess.

"Sensational," said Max.

"They were amazing," said Tess, "and they took us in. Incredibly kind, well, sort of," she added.

Anna laughed. "Yes, I could agree with that. Mostly they're *very* kind, but they can be a little, well, 'bratty' is not the right word . . . 'daring.' And I don't just mean daring. Sometimes they can almost be confrontational, in a daring kind of way. But they don't mean any harm by it. In a way, it's part of their charm. I miss that." She'd started to say "them," but she'd changed it to "that," sounding very sad and wistful as she said it. "I miss that easy way we had of playing, even when we were performing a high-wire trapeze act. It was always a little like playing . . . I miss them." This time she said what she meant.

The black horse locked Tess in a stare, and she felt compelled to wander over and touch the horse's nose softly. The horse bowed her head.

The owner of the traveller's wagon was outside, too. Julian. He laughed when he saw Tess playing with the horse. "She needs a good riding," he said to Tess, almost as if *he* was tempting her. "She's a show horse," said Julian. He corrected himself. "She *was* a show horse. I retired 'er. She is made for better things than pulling this trailer. But I trailer 'er when we travel long distances."

Somehow that made Max feel better. If the horse was "trailered" when they went long distances, in other words she was put in a horse trailer that was pulled down the street or highway attached to a car, then maybe, maybe they were in this century, after all.

Tess was stroking the horse's nose again, both her and the horse's eyes locked in a loving stare.

"She likes you," said Julian. "She doesn't like everyone. Sometimes she can be quite a handful."

"My dad says that about Tess sometimes, too," said Max.

"Max!" said Tess, sort of annoyed.

"Sorry," said Max, "but he does . . ."

"Julian, I want to introduce my new friends Tess and Max," said Anna. "They know Alexei and Tatiana."

"Really?" said Julian. "They know the twins. I would say that's odd or . . . coincidental."

It was funny to hear *coincidence* used that way . . . As if coincidence was a quirk, or luck, or an unlikely twist of fate that seemed sort of improbable. From what Tess knew about England and their past experiences, there were high odds, as Aunt Evie would say, of having a coincidence.

She looked at Julian inquisitively, trying to figure out what she thought his relationship was to Anna. *Guardian.* That was what she'd called him. What did she and Max know? *That Anna had been rented out to another carnival. That part was clear and this was probably the carnival she'd been rented out to.* Wasn't it?

It was equally hard for Tess to guess Julian's age. He was tanned from the sun but had almost no lines on his face, so it was difficult to tell if he was twenty-five or fifty or older. He had long brown, almost chestnut-colored hair that fell straight to his shoulders. It was clean and shiny, though, almost as if it had been blown dry or he'd been to a beauty shop or a barber that day. His manner was friendly but a little bit distant, at least to them, so far. He looked like the type of person that didn't talk much. Her mom would probably peg him as a loner, like that guy Franny went out with for a while who used to disappear for weeks at a time and take long solo canoe trips down rivers. It was clear Julian was quite protective of Anna.

Guardian. How did he become her guardian? Tess had some questions of her own.

Tess still couldn't quite figure Julian out. He was obviously outdoorsy. He lived, at least at the moment, in a wagon, he had a horse, and he was expertly standing over a fire pit that it looked as if he'd dug himself (which he had) in the ground and lined it with stones. There were blue and yellow flames kicking up over the rocks, and a makeshift grill had been placed over it.

There were metal folding chairs, painted deep green, quite heavy as if they were made out of cast iron. Their color almost blended in with the deep green grassy field where they were placed just outside the old-fashioned wagon, and the chairs had iron legs that ended in elaborate silver six-pointed stars. The chairs' legs seemed to have a sprinkling of glitter in the silver paint, and they sparkled, not a lot but just enough to be noticeable.

Tess whispered to Max, "Magical outdoor furniture?" But Max didn't laugh. He'd almost had enough of magic for the day.

There was a square dining table with similar legs, the six-pointed glittery stars, three points up, three points down, and almost rectangular, oddly shaped for a star. And who could guess what the top of the table looked like, as it was covered in a white-and-red checked table-cloth. Tess noted it was cotton. She also noticed that Julian was wearing somewhat old-fashioned clothes, but it was clear he was eccentric. Or maybe that *was* the theme of the carnival. *Note to self: ask Anna what the theme of the carnival is.*

"Really? You know Alexei and Tatiana?" Julian repeated, after thinking about it for way more than a minute. "And how did you come to know them?" he asked. For a moment, he sounded very British or else he was playing with them.

"It's a long story," said Max.

"A little complex," added Tess.

"Really," said Julian. It was more like a statement than a question. "I'm quite sure Anna and I would both love to hear it."

the story according to tess and max, or at least what they told to julian and anna

Tess told the story and Max just listened quietly as his sister was sort of a master at it. Telling a story and leaving out parts that she thought might get them in trouble or be difficult to explain.

"We met them at another carnival," she said. That part was true. "We saw them perform. And we, well, we liked them so much. Actually I met Alexei outside the blue tent and . . . and . . ." This is where it got tricky.

"Actually," said Tess, "I'm a dancer, well, sort of a dancer, I'm not professional but I'm trained, I've taken a lot of ballet and . . . and they shouldn't have, but"—she smiled a little when she said this—"he and Tatiana gave me a lesson in aerial ballet. And right before he threw me the first bar I caught, he said to me, 'Touch the sky.' That's how I recognized your autograph . . ."

Max was impressed Tess had managed to leave out the scary parts, not tell about being hypnotized, or being at one carnival and somehow ending up at another, or having the carnival move with you and then running away to another. He just let Tess go on.

"When we saw them," said Tess, "there was a poster on the side of the tent that said 'The Breathtaking Baranovas,' and there was a picture of the three of you. But there were only two of you in the act, Tatiana and Alexei. So Max and I asked, and I think they explained that you were working at another carnival for now. And here you are."

Tess was impressed she'd figured that out. Figured out how to tell a story artfully and leave out so many secrets, without having anyone suspect. She wasn't sure this was a talent she necessarily wanted to be that good at, but she did notice that, particularly when she went to England, it was a useful talent to have.

"Really," said Julian. "And how did you manage to find us here? Did your parents bring you to Wales?"

Wales. That's where they were. That made sense, sort of. Wales was across the ocean from Devon. Of course they hadn't crossed the ocean to get there.

"Wales? That's across the ocean, isn't it?" said Max.

Julian ignored the question and asked Max one instead. "And what about your parents? Where are they?" asked Julian.

Max fielded this one. "I don't think our parents know that we left." Max hoped that this was true, although he was quite certain Aunt Evie had contacted them in Barcelona by now.

Tess's mind was racing. *Was there a way to present themselves as runaways? Did she think she could get Julian to buy that?*

But before she could get further with this thought, Anna said, "It's all right. You can tell us what happened."

"What really happened," Julian added, echoing what seemed to be his favorite word. It reminded Tess of Aunt Evie. Aunt Evie often liked to say "really," too. In fact, so often that Tess and Max sometimes laughed at her when she said it, but they weren't laughing now.

Tess started at the beginning. Not the actual beginning

but from the time when they'd been dropped at the carnival by Aunt Evie. Tess told the part about the Ferris wheel getting stuck and rescuing the little boy. She fudged a little bit on the part with Tara. She didn't lie that they'd gone into the psychic trailer, but she didn't quite tell the part about getting hypnotized. But she did say, though, it was almost like the carnival ran away with them.

Tess expected them to stop her there, when she got to that part, but Julian and Anna exchanged a look that indicated this didn't surprise them at all.

She told about meeting Alexei and Tatiana and the aerial ballet lesson. She left out the part about the audience—that part seemed too strange—but she did explain about falling, free fall, missing the second bar, hurtling toward the ground, and time seeming to slow down. And then the swing dropped somehow, the pink satin swing hanging from silver ropes, and how she somersaulted into it sideways from the air.

She told them about the carnival closing for the night, being closed in, so to speak, and them not even knowing where they were.

Where had the carnival landed?

She explained how they'd spent the night in the tent with Tatiana and Alexei. And Alexei had told the story that their father used to tell to them at bedtime, which began, *Once upon a time, there was a little girl named Anoushka,* which is how Tess knew Anna's childhood name. Then she told the part about Lorenzo giving Max the crazy job at The House of Mirrors. Anna and Julian exchanged another look as if they had an understanding of what that was, too.

And then Max jumped in. "And then in the very early morning," Max said, "I took a little walk around and I found the strangest thing. Pine trees. We thought we were in the Alps. We thought that was where the carnival had landed. Tess and I went to school in Switzerland last year. But these pine trees weren't planted in the ground. They had stands like we have sometimes for Christmas trees at home. And there were sheets over them."

Anna shook her head and exchanged another look with Julian, who nodded.

"And then," asked Anna, "did Tara serve polenta griddle cakes with homemade honey?"

"Yes," said Tess and Max in unison.

Anna sighed. "Lorenzo gets lonesome for the Italian Alps. That's where he was born. And then he gets incredibly cranky. So they move the carnival a hill or two and dress the mountain up with pine trees and trick him so that he thinks they're in the Italian Alps. And he gets a little cheerier. Not much, but a little. Somehow he never catches on."

"So, we were still in Devon?"

"Yes, I think so," said Anna.

"Yes," Julian echoed. "Most likely still in Devon."

"They're still in Devon!" said Tess excitedly. And she and Max both smiled.

She went on to tell them about the morning, how after breakfast Lorenzo intended to enlist Tess, force her rather, into taking Anna's place in the aerial ballet show, The Breathtaking Baranovas. Tess explained that somehow overnight, her picture had been painted in instead of Anna's. And how frightened she was that that might somehow set her future, their future in stone.

"I'm not trained to be an aerial ballet star," said Tess, nodding humbly to Anna, "but I also had the oddest feeling that if I had, if I had even performed one real show, that neither Max or I would ever be able to leave the carnival. I didn't put this leotard on this morning," she said to Anna, "it was sort of like it put itself on me . . . when I wasn't even looking."

"And I didn't put on this carnival uniform, either," said Max, echoing his sister's fear.

Julian interrupted. "Carnival Magic can have a dark side, too," he said.

Tess thought it best not to question that, as they'd had a bit of experience with that, too.

She told the part about how Lorenzo had chased her. Calling her name. And then she remembered he'd even tried to change her name to Tessa. "He tried to change my name to Tessa. I forgot that part," she said. "That was ridiculous. The idea that *he* could change my name. The idea that *he* was going to tell me that I was going to work for him." In that moment she sounded like herself. Tess, the girl who wasn't afraid of anything. But as she said that, she could hear Lorenzo calling her. "Tess-a, Tess-a, Tess-a." The words echoing on each other. Tess took a deep breath and looked around and realized she was just hearing it in her mind. "He was chasing me.

"Then"—she hesitated—"this part won't make any sense . . . we found an opening in The House of Mirrors, and that's how we ended up here."

Neither Anna or Julian seemed at all surprised by this last bit.

"Max found it, actually," said Tess, giving her brother the proper credit. "And Alexei was an enormous amount of help." Tess sighed because she realized that she missed him.

"And then," Max cut in, "Tess held a needle up."

Were they going to ask her to explain the needle?

"Where did you get the needle, Tess?" asked Max, as if anticipating her anxiety.

"If I told you I pulled it out of a baby tiger's paw, would you believe me?"

"Yes," said Max, showing amazing sibling stripes, "I probably would." Neither Anna or Julian questioned this answer, either.

The moon was out now, and there were stars. Galaxies of them. Almost as if the dark blue sky had sparkling polka dots in varying sizes.

"I don't understand something," Max said, looking at Julian. "How come Anna has a guardian and the twins, Tatiana and Alexei, don't?"

"But the twins do have a guardian," said Julian. "They always have. Tara. Tara's their guardian. Actually she's all of their guardians. I just volunteered when it was clear Lorenzo was going to send Anna away. She couldn't go by herself. And Lorenzo insisted on keeping the twins there."

Tess ran back through all of it in her mind and realized that she and Max had been alone with Tara only once in the psychic wagon, but that was a few hours before Tatiana and Alexei were scheduled to perform. She realized whenever they'd been with Alexei and Tatiana, showing up backstage and sewing the star on the leotard; setting the tent up; turning the beds down; appearing at breakfast with the polenta cakes, Tara had always been there watching over them.

"I know, Tara's a curious choice for a guardian," said Julian. "But then again, you could probably say that I'm a curious choice for a guardian, too."

the seven estry

They invented the language," said Max. "How come no one can pronounce anything properly?" It was a fairly rude statement, and Max was somewhat relieved when Julian laughed. Julian was speaking to them about the Seven Estry.

The Seven Estry.

That wasn't what it was called at all. That was just what it sounded like when Julian said it.

It was actually the Severn Estuary, which is a geographical designation.

An estuary is where a river runs into the sea. And the Severn Estuary is where the River Severn, the largest river in England, runs into the sea at the very top of the Bristol Channel that borders both England on one side and Wales on the other. *Yes, they really were in Wales, it seemed.*

So, in answer to the question that they'd asked before—was there any way to get back to Devon across the sea?—the answer was one that might be called a hard yes.

There was a lot to consider.

There was the distinct possibility that if Tess and Max stayed at The Ghost Carnival, they might never be able to leave. What if they were enlisted as workers there, too?

There was the unknown factor of what might happen to them or where they would be if they left through the outside gate of The Ghost Carnival. Max and Tess had had an experience like this before, where it was almost as if they'd stepped off the edge of the world. And both Tess and Max agreed, if it were possible to avoid this, they would definitely prefer it!

Not that they might not have already stepped off the edge of the world just by going through the pane of glass, but at least the sky still looked the same, at least there were stars. And people seemed to have barbecued dinner and drink orange drinks.

Julian explained to them that from where the wagon was parked, *if* they went the other direction, away from the carnival, they'd get to the coast. There was a beach there. Not without its own risks and dangers. But at least there was a shoreline onto the sea, and on the other side of the sea was England. The northwest side of Devon, not the southeast, but at least they might have a shot at crossing the land and getting back to South Devon . . . assuming they were able to cross that bit of the ocean.

There were apparently a number of remarkable things about the Seven Estry. The beach and the tide and the Bristol Channel itself, which fed into the Atlantic Ocean, had a few remarkable distinguishing characteristics.

At one point in the day (or two points sometimes) on the beach, the tide was so low that when it went out, you couldn't even see the sea from the sand. Such a long stretch of sand that it almost seemed as if you were on a desert. And then when the tide came in again, they said it came in like "a galloping horse." High, mighty, with enormous riptides and other terrifying complications. "It's thought to have the highest surge waves in the world—they call them tidal bores," said Julian. "A tidal bore is when a wave breaks so high because the tide is coming in so quickly," he explained. "Well, maybe the second highest now. I think there's one in Australia that might be higher."

At least that was the way Julian explained it to them.

"We're a little south here," he said, "not quite sure how far south, so the ocean's a little tamer here, but it can be quite rough."

Julian seemed to be suggesting this as an escape route, a way to get back to England, a way to get back to Devon, but somehow they'd have to cross the sea.

"We might be down by Swansea," said Julian. "I'm not really sure. Alberto doesn't give us a road map."

The fact that Julian didn't quite know where they were didn't give Max a big boost of confidence on their chances, and when Julian added this next bit, it didn't help at all. "You have to fight the undercurrent," said Julian. "You know, that thing when you get hit by a wave. And you have no idea what *these* waves are like. Riptide. It pulls you under when the wave breaks and starts to roll back from the shore. It pulls you under and takes you along."

Max remembered two summers ago in Long Island, after a rainstorm, he tried to bodysurf, and the surf was so high and crazy that he got flipped around, and knocked under a wave. And Max knew enough about oceans and surfing to know that most people consider the tides in Long Island to be kindergarten.

Tess remembered, too, because they'd been alone, without their parents, on the beach. An older boy who'd been swimming had seen it happen and helped Max back to shore. Tess was already swimming out to him. But the boy got to him first. Tess remembered that they hadn't even asked his name. They thanked him. But they hadn't even asked his name.

"Riptide?" said Tess. "And tidal bores?" She wasn't sure she was up for riptides. Riptides and tidal bores seemed particularly unpredictable.

"And then there's another problem," Julian added. "There's so much mud—famous mudflats some places. Up at the top for sure, north of here. It's peculiar mud. It almost seems to have a mind of its own. People who've survived it say it reaches up and grabs you. And some of them say that they've seen strange creatures in the mud."

Tess and Max exchanged a look now, wondering if they were really up for strange creatures in the mud . . .

Of course there were, thought Tess to herself. *Of course there would be strange creatures that would try to grab you.*

"We're not really in the mood to be grabbed," said Tess definitively, as if just by saying it, she could prevent it. And she reached her finger out to Max and executed a pinkie swear.

Julian hesitated, as if he wasn't certain he should tell them this next part. "People have been known to sink into it." The way he said this kind of indicated that they might not have ever been seen again.

What were your chances if you happened to sink into it? Max wasn't sure he was a strong enough swimmer to take that chance. He looked at Tess to see what she thought. Tess was looking at Anna.

"But, there's a ton of windsurfers there, in England, anyway," Julian added, "braving the sea every day."

Max wasn't sure he had a certificate in windsurfing. He was pretty good on a skateboard, but he'd never really tried to even stand up on a boogie board on a wave . . . His sister, Tess, usually thought she could do anything.

"But like you said, we're a little south of the Severn Estuary," said Tess to Julian. "You're just not sure how far south? And if we can cross, it'll get us back to Devon?"

"Well, it will get you back to England, and then you'll have to cross the land to get to Devon. But, if you can cross the sea, it most definitely will get you back to the western coast of England," said Julian. "It most certainly will."

Was it the sort of thing you flip a coin on? *Whether to cross the sea or not?*

Of course, they'd decided they would be on horseback. But Tess wondered what guaranteed that the horse could swim.

"That she can," said Julian, as if he could read Tess's thoughts. "She's a funny one," he said, looking lovingly at the horse. "And she loves to swim."

Why couldn't they just walk out the door and find their way to town and take a train? Max thought this to himself and didn't say it out loud.

But it was as if Julian had heard Max. "Do you really think that would work, Max?" asked Julian, as he picked up his violin. "Can I remind you of the route you took to find your way here?"

It was decided then. Tess and Max would take the ebony-colored horse, who Julian said came from a long line of champions. Tess had already friended her.

"We discussed it," said Anna. "It was Julian's idea that you take the horse. But please try to take care of her. Julian's actually quite fond of her."

Julian almost teared up at that. He placed his violin

on his shoulder. He started to play, softly at first, and then the sound got louder, brighter somehow, a sort of haunting melody that echoed across the hills, single multi-pitched tones, pure, rich, multifaceted tones that latched into a melody with highs and lows and in-betweens, as if it was the soundtrack to a story.

the first farewell

4:06 a.m. That was the exact time Julian gently shook them—very gently—by their shoulders to wake them, which they did in an instant, as sleep had been difficult to come by the night before.

Tess had slept fitfully, her body already tensed as if it was in training for the journey ahead. Meanwhile, Max's mind had been racing so quickly he questioned whether he'd had any sleep at all. He kept running scenarios of *so* many things that could go wrong . . .

But Tess was game for it, determined, and he had no choice but to go along. Also, practically speaking, Max wasn't sure they had another option except to try.

Sunrise was calculated to be 5:01, at least according to a year-old guide printed on an oversized paper that Julian had from the summer before. The plan was to be on the beach at eight minutes to five. 4:52 a.m. exactly: a long enough time to survey; not long enough to get frightened. At least that was the calculus Julian had suggested the night before.

Julian had packed them a canteen of water, a bar of dark chocolate wrapped in silver foil, biscuits, English crackers, a wedge of white cheese, and two oranges, wrapped in a cloth as if that would somehow protect them from the ocean.

"You always have to have an orange when you're goin' to sea," said Julian. As if it was a superstition that you could get scurvy or something. *Scurvy was a disease that sailors used to get on long ocean crossings from getting no vitamin C.* Tess remembered that from history class, but she couldn't remember if it was about Christopher Columbus or the *Mayflower*.

Tess felt she should be able to remember that, but she

had so many other things on her mind. She'd never ridden the ebony horse. She knew they had a bond. But what if the horse was skittish, not used to taking direction? Julian had kind of intimated that the horse could be a bit wild. Tess didn't want to frighten Max. But she made a *Note to self: tell Max to hold on very tightly as we ride.*

Max wished he had a compass. Julian didn't have one. Max had asked.

Max's iPhone had a compass on it, but both his and Tess's phones had been out of battery for at least twenty-four hours (or was it days?). There wasn't electricity at the traveller's wagon. Max had asked that, too. So, all they had was the horse as their only means of transportation, and the shore and the sky as their only directional bench-marks. Max wished he had a map so he could see exactly what direction they were heading but figured when the sun came up at least they'd know that was east.

Not that that would do a lot of good if he didn't know what latitude and longitude they were actually aiming toward. And with the apparent reputation of the coast of Wales, with its wild tides and undertows, Max was more than frightened they could be lost at sea.

"Anna and I will walk you to the top hill, just above the sand," said Julian, "and I'll draw a map for you to sort of show you where you are and hopefully where you're heading." That Julian had added "sort of" and "hopefully" didn't give Max a lot of confidence.

"That would be great," said Tess, elbowing Max when she said it. "Thank you."

No matter what happened, Julian was trying to help them and it was always right to say thank you.

The horse was saddled and ready. Anna had put a ribbon on the horse's mane. Anna kissed the back of the horse's neck and handed the reins to Tess. "Take care of her," she said to Tess. "I can't wait till the day when I can ride her again."

Julian had packed an apple cut in fours, and he told Tess the apple was for the horse along with a little sack filled with something that looked like Cheerios. Though how Julian expected them to try to feed the horse at sea was beyond Tess's understanding. So Tess took it to mean that Julian was quite confident in their ability to succeed and it was for when they reached the beach on the English shore.

"Aren't you coming with us?" Tess asked, "at least to see us off at the sand?"

"No," said Julian, "we don't do that. We'll only go as far as the hill above the beach. Anna's not really allowed to leave the carnival grounds. But you knew that, too, didn't you, Tess?"

Tess looked puzzled, and Anna tried to lighten it. "Stop scaring them, Julian. I doubt that the tide is really as crazy as he says." And she further explained, although Tess wasn't sure she believed the explanation, "Alberto always brings us breakfast, and if we're not there, he'll come after us for sure. And who knows what would happen to you. They promised me, six months more on my contract and then I can leave."

Tess wondered if this was true, if Anna ever was going to be allowed to leave. What did Julian mean when he said Anna wasn't allowed to leave the carnival grounds? What would happen if she did? But there wasn't any time left to wonder.

They followed Julian, who was holding the horse's reins. He stopped occasionally to lovingly pat her nose. Tess caught him giving her a sugar cube. Tess wondered how long the horse had been Julian's and thought it was incredibly generous of Julian to "lend her" to them. That was the way Tess chose to think of it, anyway; that Julian was loaning the horse to them and one day they would all be reunited. That was the only positive way to think about this.

At the very top of the hill, Julian stopped. Beneath

them, there was a path through the woods partly covered with heath and brush that was so wild it was difficult to see where it led or how to find your way through it.

"Don't worry," said Julian, "she knows the rest of the path. I let her run free sometimes—sometimes there's a silver layer of sand she leaves in the dirt when she returns. Isn't there?" he said to the horse, as if the horse could understand him. "And salt water in your mane. You've run in the sand and been swimming in this sea before." He patted her nose again, but this time like he was saying farewell, not good-bye, certainly not good-bye, but good journey. "Travel safely," he said, looking into the horse's eyes as he said it.

"It's just straight there," he said to Tess, pointing to a road barely visible in the overgrown field, running the opposite way from the carnival, across and down the hill, and presumably on to the sea. "No turns," he said insistently, "even if one appears to you. If you take it straight, it leads directly to the sea."

Tess and Max looked at Anna, but neither of them knew exactly what to say. Anna started speaking first, though. "I want to tell you how much I admire you," said Anna. "I don't often get to say that to people. I don't often feel that."

Max was almost blushing, as he thought Anna's achievements (and he hadn't even see her do any aerial ballet, just wing walking) were quite astonishing. And it was clear she'd risked her life for the twins.

But then Max realized that Anna was speaking to Tess, almost like they were sisters or shared a secret bond. Tess answered with just one word. "Ditto," she said. She held her pinkie up and Anna held up hers and they did a pinkie swear.

"You, too," said Anna, looking at Max. And both Anna and Tess nodded to Max, and he put his pinkie up, too, and joined in as if it were a three-way oath, held up righteously toward the sky.

Julian interrupted gruffly, "We all have that in common. Get on with it. We're trying to beat a sunrise, remember." But when Tess looked at him, she saw that it seemed as if he had a couple of tears in his eyes.

Anna began to speak hurriedly. "Tell them, Tatiana and Alexei, that I'm fine," she said. "Tell them that. And don't tell them anything else. Tell them that Julian's with me and he's taking quite good care of me, sort of." She couldn't help this last bit, but Julian smiled. "Don't— do not—tell them about the wing walking, even though I know both Alexei and Tatiana would be jealous, it would worry them all the same. Six months, they've promised, and then we'll be together again."

Tess wondered who had promised this. If Anna was counting on Alberto or Lorenzo?

"I'm sure of it," said Anna. "They promised. So give this," she said, "to each of them. To Tatiana and Alexei." And she kissed both Tess and Max gently on their foreheads. "And tell them that I send them love and I can't wait until we're together again and we can touch the sky."

Tess nodded and held a pinkie up to Anna again and did a version of a pinkie swear without linking fingers, just a symbolic one, a brave one, a triumphant one, held up in the air. Then Max did the same, a symbolic solid pinkie swear, onward, a link between them that signified their bond would last forever.

"Thank you," Tess said to Julian. And then she said to Anna, "Don't worry, together we *will* touch the sky."

Tess mounted first. She felt secure, at ease, almost at one with the horse. That was a relief. The horse was totally attuned to her. Tess leaned down and whispered in the horse's ear, and the horse turned slyly, tossing her mane, and locked her eye for a moment with Tess, as if to let her know she understood.

Julian helped Max onto the saddle behind Tess. "Hold

on tight, Max," said Tess. "Hold on very tight." Max put his arms around his sister's waist. Max turned and looked back at Anna and put his left hand up in the air.

"Her name's Coco, by the way," said Julian to Tess, "in case you didn't figure that out yet." Julian gave Coco a light pat on her hind leg, and before Tess could even answer him, Coco took off on a path that strangely only did become visible as you ran through it, which Coco did at breakneck speed.

Of course her name was Coco. Why hadn't Tess figured that out before? And Julian really did look a lot like the gentleman they'd met in Devon when the carnival was first setting up, the gentleman with the traveller's wagon and the horse named Coco, the gentleman who'd talked to them about the six-pointed star on the black airplane and said it might be an equation for an alternate universe. Of course, he'd told them that. Tess wanted to stop and talk to Max about this, but Coco wasn't having any stopping, she was cantering. Something even faster than a canter, straight down the path, racing towards the beach.

waiting for high tide

The beach was breathtaking. They saw it from above at first as Coco led them down the beach path. And then they were on the sand. The sand was brown with bright flecks of silver and specks of white sparkling, as if hundreds of shells had shattered against the cliffs and shore.

The tide was out now and, as described, out so far that you couldn't even see the sea.

They'd dismounted and were standing on the beach.

Max picked up a seashell and put it to his ear to see if he could hear the sea from it, but even it was silent. Tess stroked Coco's mane and gave her a slice of apple. Tess opened the canteen and allowed Max to have a sip, just one and one sip only, and did the same. They started to hear something, far away and then closer.

Everything looked to Tess as if it was almost in black-and-white with tiny hints of brown and silver.

She started to run different sequences through her mind.

What if they were able to cross the sea? What if they were separated from Coco with the force of a wave or current? What if there were creatures or mudflats below them? And then when, if they reached the other side, could they make the trip to Devon, and try to find where the carnival was, where it had landed?

It was still in Devon. She was sure of it.

If they could get back in time. In time for what? What a funny expression that was. How long would the journey take?

But Tess reasoned they had to get away. She and Max had to get away. She thought there was a danger they would be stuck there. *Forever. She didn't know what that meant.* She didn't know why she thought that, but she did.

Well, it made sense. What if that carnival, Fun Fair as they called it, decided to move? Where would they be then? And what would they be wearing? They had to get back to Aunt Evie. To Devon-by-the-Sea. Their parents must be worried sick by now. And if they went back to try to rescue Anna, they might never get away . . . That was the first time that occurred to her—if they tried to rescue Anna . . .

Tess helped Max lift his foot into the stirrup and stood by him as he threw his other leg over and reseated himself in the saddle. She jumped on herself almost in one continuous motion in front of him. She grabbed the reins securely.

But the thing that was nagging at her now was, how could they go back to Alexei and Tatiana without Anna? They'd found her. That was the miracle in itself. But they had to get away, and time was not their friend here. Once they were back in Devon, they would figure it out. Their parents would help them figure it out.

Tess leaned down and whispered to Coco. "You are my steed and I am your Knight and together we will succeed." She held the reins firmly in her hands.

"Hold on to me, Max. Hold on to me tight," said Tess.

The sound of the ocean was practically deafening. They still couldn't see even the start of the sea, not even foam. Just a bare beach, as if there'd been a horrible accident.

Still. No sign of the sea.

But then the texture of the sand started to change as if there was water below the ground. Cracks and crevices opening. Mud, splatters of mud, reaching around the horse's hooves and ankles.

Max was mesmerized by the mud and was starting to see shapes form in it. Creatures. He had to be imagining it.

The mouths of crocodiles. An eel-like thing that seemed to tie itself in ropes, black and slinky. Max wondered if it was the equivalent of a boa constrictor in the sea. Next up, the long neck and large mouth of a King cobra snake jutting up from the sand, the skin of which had crazy triangular patterns, which got smaller as they fluttered down to a mermaid-like tail, more frightening because of its antic swirl, enticing and dangerous. Its mouth open, emitting a high-pitched tone almost like a flute. He must be imagining it, he reasoned. He must just be seeing patterns in the sand. He was letting his imagination run away with itself. Or was he?

"Don't look down," Tess said to Max. "Just don't look down." But Max ignored her and swatted at what he was sure was the singing snake-like thing, kicking it sharply with his heel, just as it was about to hiss and lock its mouth on Coco's right hind leg. Direct hit. With a sound almost like a whimper and a quiet hiss, it disappeared under the dirtlike sand, where Max hoped it was going to stay for a while.

There was what looked like a large clamshell, peaceful, serene, but when it opened its top, something like an evil-black seahawk's head popped out, its beak open and ready to strike.

Tess screamed. Max instinctively put his hand over her mouth to stop her scream. And she took a deep breath and held it. But it was as if the scream had done its just job, frightened the evil-black seahawk, and the clamshell's top flipped down again and remained peaceful and serene. For the moment, anyway.

Max remembered that he still had in his pocket the curious stopwatch—the one that counted down (or up) to seven minutes. He was relieved to know it wasn't ticking now.

Max looked behind him and saw, perhaps the scariest of all, a tortoise that seemed to be resting in the sand, so benign and wise, and gentle, its brown-and-white shell shiny and almost sparkly. But then it lifted itself on its front legs, flipped over, seeming to grow to three feet tall, and revealed that it was actually a giant tarantula, legs waving menacingly, waiting to unleash its venom. Coco seemed to sense that it was there even though it was behind her and kicked her back hooves into the sand, again and again, covering it, dousing it, completely burying it from sight. Coco then ground down the sand with her back hoof as if to secure it, compact it, hold the sand in place, pounding her hoof over and over to permanently keep the terrible gigantic spider, if it was a spider or something even more sinister, underneath the ground.

The sun began to rise at the horizon line in the distance, still no hint of the sea, just flat rays reflecting across the land and bright light reflecting across the glittery sand. It was the crack of dawn. And even though the sun was rising, everything still looked as if it was in black-and-white . . . with added shades of brown.

Tess remembered the way her bedroom looked that first morning in the attic at the cottage in Devon-by-the-Sea, almost as if it was in black-and-white. And wondered now if that was a foretelling of the future, but she pushed the thought away. Tess reasoned, there wasn't actually any color on the beach, the dark sand with its flecks of white, the cliffs hovering over the beach creating their own form of darkness, white shells, even the bits of seaweed left behind looked brown instead of green.

Still, despite the mud and the water bubbling up from crevices, there was still no sign of the coming sea or any body of land on the other side.

How far away was the coast of England? Her mind was racing now. *What if they did cross the sea? Then they had to make the journey across the land to South Devon . . . and hope that the carnival was still there and that they could find it . . .*

And then, it was as if she was seeing Alexei and Tatiana's faces in front of her. Not really their faces, more like the dance they did in the sky.

Then Tess had a vision of Anna grabbing the ring, flying to reach her brother's arms, as Tatiana sat in the moon, smiling, and watched them. It was as if Tess was seeing an image or imagining a movie. But she couldn't shake the image. *Anna. Anna grabbing the ring. Was that why they'd been sent here? Was there a reason, after all?*

The sand was quickly turning to layers of mud that were so thick it was like quicksand below them. It occurred to Tess they could sink in it at any moment and never be seen again.

Strange dark tentacles of mud, or were they creatures, seeming to reach out for them.

The sound of the coming wave was almost deafening. And still they couldn't see it.

What was it they said? *Comes in like a galloping horse.*

Tess wondered, what if the wave came in and they hit it at the wrong angle or tried to ride the wrong crest or couldn't connect to the flow of the tide? They could be crashed against the rocks themselves. The cliff was foreboding. And so was the sight of the beachscape without any sign of the sea.

The sound was growing now, like the sound of a wave in a seashell blasting through an amplifier, deafeningly reverberating against the cliffs, echoing, as the white tops of the waves racing toward them were suddenly frighteningly evident far off in the beginning waters of the sea.

Coco was ready, poised, tense, as if she knew exactly what she was to do. A show horse, showing all her colors, her neck held high, tapping a little with her right hoof as if she couldn't wait to take off.

But then Tess knew with certainty the reason why they couldn't cross. *They couldn't leave Anna here. If there was a reason they'd been sent here.* Their mom believed that sometimes there was a reason for everything. *But how would they get Anna back?*

And then her father's words came back to her. It was something that he always said. "If you get lost, go back to where you started if you can." He always added that part,

"If you can." Go back to where you started, if you can.

The force of the ocean was pulling the sand beneath them, and pulling them with it, starting to force them out to sea as the waves were about to reach them.

The rivulets of mud were popping higher now, as if they were coils, like snakes wrapping around the horse's legs and seeming to bake like concrete, holding her legs down. Coco, her pedigree showing bright, was kicking her heels to try to stay clear of it.

Tess gripped the reins as the ocean started to race inevitably towards them and tried to pick them up in its wake.

Tess gripped the reins tightly with her right hand and turned Coco's neck as she did so, digging her knees into the horse's side, nudging her to turn and at the same time, trying to hold on.

"Hold on to me, Max. Hold on. There's no way we can do this. We can't leave Anna here."

Go back to where you started if you can.

She yanked at the reins again, almost harder than she meant to, trying to turn Coco around. And Coco obediently turned and instantly sped into a run, a run away from the twenty-foot wave that looked as if it was thirty feet high that was galloping towards them.

The mud pulled them in, deeper and deeper as she ran, and Coco fell, almost to her right knee, as the first wash of water swept over them. Tess knelt over the horse's neck—she wasn't sure where she got the strength—and pulled Coco's leg from the mud. Tess held her breath as she looked up as the enormous wave crested and fell like an entire ocean around them.

Tess never lost her grip. "You are my steed. And I am your Knight, and we will be victorious," she whispered again into Coco's ear as the wave rolled wildly over them, washing them under. And there was nothing to see but the sea.

It was Coco who broke the water first. Her head, then her neck, her mane dripping water, gasping for air with a high-pitched whine that deepened finally into a neigh, a horse's sigh of relief, as Coco, mouth open wide, took a huge breath of air into her lungs. Tess's face was visible, just the side of her face, lying flat, her cheek up against Coco's mane, lying flat on the horse, holding the reins, holding the saddle, as she tried to keep her mount, and Max seated behind her, bravely holding on to Tess's waist, his legs, too, firmly gripped to Coco.

The horse was swimming, but it wasn't really a swim. It was a thoroughbred canter through the waves, backward as the wave was going out now and they were trying to go in. Faster and faster she ran, Tess holding on and keeping clear sight between the horse's ears, gently guiding her now and urging her to run on.

It was a sight, if there had been anyone there to see. The race of a champion, a majestic feat, as Coco ran through the enormous wave and brought them back to the barely visible shore.

But there was no stopping here. The sun was rising rapidly in the sky. The carnival would soon again begin. Tess imagined the biplanes were almost ready. A line of carnival-goers outside the gate.

"Faster, Coco. Faster still," Tess begged as she tapped the horse's sides with her heels and they ran faster still. Onto the road, the almost hidden road, through the fields dotted with wildflowers and heather, so quickly that the purple heather was almost a blur of violet across the land. When they reached the top of the hill, Coco executed a jump as if there was a hedge. It sounded for a moment as if the ground was crackling. Max held on to Tess, and Coco gracefully landed back on flatter ground. And they were on the top of the hill where Julian and Anna had last left them.

Coco never broke her pace, winding swiftly on the

road as it zigged down the hill again to flat land and back to the traveller's wagon . . . only to find that the wagon was gone and there was no one there at all.

Tess dismounted. She looked around to see if she could see anything at all. But there was nothing, just heath and grass and wildflowers, still pale as if everything was in watercolor tones. Washed-out watercolor tones.

She gave Coco a sip of water, awkwardly, from the canteen, much of it spilling down Coco's long neck but much appreciated. Tess stroked Coco's neck. She could feel the sweat beneath Coco's mane. "Just a little longer," she whispered in Coco's ear, and as she said it, she hoped that it was true.

If they followed the road, would they find them? Followed the road back to The Ghost Carnival. That's what Tess was calling it now in her mind. *The Ghost Carnival.*

"Don't drink too much," she said to Max as she handed him the canteen and put her foot in the stirrup again to take her mount. Max took a sip and handed it back to Tess, successfully seated in front of him now. She took a sip, and Max put the canteen back in the saddlebag.

"Just a little further now," Tess whispered again to Coco as she lightly gave the horse a tap with both of her heels, holding the reins back as she did it. "Slowly. We have to go very slowly now. Slow and steady. So that nobody will hear us."

They travelled back through the path that led to where they were the day before, the airfield, the olive grove. In the distance, they could see the biplanes were ready on the runway. But no sign of any of the other aviators. *Were they already in the planes?* A crowd of onlookers had started to gather. *Were they already too late?* Tess was certain they wouldn't be able to hide in plain sight as they'd done the day before. Alberto would certainly recognize them.

And just as she was about to give up hope, she saw them from the back, walking just ahead. Anna already in her pilot's uniform, Julian at her side.

Tess jumped off the horse and instructed Max to do the same, and they ran together, Tess holding Coco's reins so that she followed just behind them.

"We couldn't leave without you," said Tess, the moment they were next to Anna.

"I didn't think you could do," said Julian, sounding peculiarly British again and as if he'd predicted it all along.

the alternate house of mirrors

Yes, there is," said Julian. "If you and Max can remember how to find it."

The decision had been made in an instant. Tess and Max and Anna and Julian would try (*try* being the operative word) to get back through The House of Mirrors. All they had to do was find that pane. How hard could that be?

"It isn't here," said Tess, staring off into the distance and not seeing anything at all.

"It has to still be there," Max insisted. But he couldn't help thinking, *Unless the carnival had moved again.*

He turned and looked carefully behind him at the olive grove they'd first seen when they entered. He traced the skyline with his eye to remember the flight of the planes and where they were when he first saw Anna wing walking. He stepped backward eight paces, counting as he did so and . . . ran directly into it, even though there didn't appear to be anything there. It was as if he'd backed into an invisible wall . . . He turned around and lightly kicked it with his foot. And his foot hit a surface, but there didn't seem to be anything there.

It wasn't quite invisible, as when they all stared at it intently, he and Tess and Anna and Julian could each see their images faintly, very faintly, reflected against the cool, smooth, oddly almost invisible surface.

Was anyone after them? It was hard to tell. The propellers of the biplanes were spinning, warming up, almost ready for their take-off. It would only be a few moments, if it hadn't happened already, that Alberto would discover, or someone would discover and tell Alberto that Anna was a "no-show."

Would they search the trailer first, or would all the carnival workers take off like individual groups of search parties in all different directions?

Max did the calculation in his mind. He grabbed Anna's hand and started to guide her into the invisible wall. Max hit his nose and almost fell backward, but Anna, who was standing right next to him, slipped right in. Max was just an inch away, and he pushed Julian in behind Anna.

Tess grabbed Max's finger in a congratulatory pinkie swear and walked with him into what they expected to be the other carnival . . . And instead found themselves in a House of Mirrors at The Ghost Carnival, an alternate House of Mirrors, if you will.

They hadn't been counting on that.

Tess realized they'd left Coco behind. Julian, as if sensing her thought, said, "Don't worry about her. She has her ways. Coco's very good on the moors. She's very good at finding her way." And then he added curiously, "The trick is not to say good-bye. That way you might have a chance of seeing each other again." Tess realized he was as sad about it as she was.

Tess and Julian both looked over and got a glimpse of Coco starting to gallop away from them as the invisible wall became dark and murky, and then, there was no way to see through it, at all.

It had not occurred to them, though, that they were

going to enter an alternate House of Mirrors. Somehow they thought they'd be able to go straight through the glass back to where they'd started. Well, sort of where they started. Back at least to the carnival where they'd last seen Alexei and Tatiana.

Max worried that maybe it was one of those funny one-way doors. Like you could see in but you couldn't see out. Like a police interrogation glass. But in this case, a one-way door, that you could go out but you couldn't get back in. He voiced this to Tess and reminded her the mirror had closed up behind them. Tess didn't want to think about that. And neither did Max, really.

Maybe they weren't in the exact spot, the exact pane of glass where the image of the other carnival had appeared on the other side and frightened the carnival-goers.

Max reasoned that that was what it was: they had to find the inverse spot, the other side of the glass, so to speak, of exactly the place where people screamed when they thought they saw the ghost images. Then, maybe they could get back in. The place Lorenzo had directed Max to where people screamed.

The alternate House of Mirrors was strange, almost cave-like, if a cave can be geometrical. It had sharp edges, jagged triangular ceilings, corridors that seemed to unexpectedly transition from wide to skinny as you walked them. The only thing straight was the floor, except that it had fissures of steam shooting up from it, creating a virtual haze. The mirrors weren't exact. They, too, were sort of hazed, and distorted their images frighteningly. Julian cautioned them not to look at their own images, not to be frightened by what they saw. "Keep your eyes directly in front of you," he said, which was pretty good advice except that the corridors in the alternate House of Mirrors twisted and turned and stopped abruptly. And Max wondered how he could be expected to find the right pane of glass, the one that led back to the other carnival, if he didn't scan the mirrors. *Well, they weren't even quite mirrors, the images in them were almost three-dimensional.* Max was even frightened they might start to emote on their own. That he'd just be standing there and his image in the glass would smile at him or worse.

Max took the lead.

Big mistake. He ran them right into a dead end in the alternate House of Mirrors.

Things in the mirror were reversed, right? Was he going the wrong way? The mirrors themselves were also murky—the reflections weren't that crisp, but they still bounced off one another, creating a ghostly spectre of reflections, multiples of all of them, scary, ominous, as if they were in a haunted house.

Anna took the lead. "I think I know the way," she said, "now that we're in." She made a right turn and walked them down a long corridor edged with glass on all sides, and then a left, and guided them into another dead-end.

Not a good sign, thought Tess, *when you can see a distorted version of your own reflection about to run into you. A head-on collision with a version of yourself.*

"Don't think we want to be playing chicken," said Julian, kind of stating the obvious as they could hear footsteps running after them, multiples of footsteps, and a voice that sounded like Alberto calling, "Anna-a. Anna-a. I know you're in there."

"It's only me they want," said Anna. "You go ahead," she said to Tess and Max. "Julian, you'll say that you were chasing me. That you saw me try to run away and then you ran after me. They'll believe me. They'll believe you, if you lie."

"I've never been that big on lying," Julian said. "It doesn't suit me somehow."

"Well, then you'll just be silent," said Anna, "you're awfully good at that. I didn't mean that," said Anna. "I'm sorry. I didn't mean that, at all."

Julian didn't seem to react except to get quieter.

The footsteps, though, were getting closer, louder.

Then Tess saw something in the shadows. Well, not really in the shadows. She saw the image of a baby tiger walking on the other side of the glass. As if it was at the real carnival, at the real House of Mirrors, on the other side of the glass. What Tess thought of as the right side. Or at least the side where they belonged. She saw a baby tiger walking. She was sure of it. Tess saw the baby tiger put a paw up. And bow her head down as if beckoning Tess to follow her.

"I know the way," Tess said to the others. "I'm certain of it."

Max looked in the glass and saw it, too. He ran to keep up with Tess, who was racing along with the tiger.

Anna ran after her, and Julian had no choice except to start to sprint after them, as he hadn't quite started walking when they did and was following a bit behind.

The glass was still murky. Almost playing tricks on Tess. One moment, she saw what looked like a baby tiger, or certainly a cat running along on the other side of the glass, and then the density was so great and so distorted, she couldn't see anything, at all. Then the tiger disappeared . . . or did it? It showed back up again. And showed her it was making a right turn. Tess turned with it. She and the baby tiger were walking in step even though they were on opposite sides of the glass.

Max was counting then, each step. And when the tiger stopped, Max said, "Scream, Tess. Scream as loud as you can," said Max. "And Anna, you scream, too. Scream high, in the highest soprano pitch you can."

The two of them screamed. And the stopwatch started ticking. They could all hear it, underneath the screams, like a metronome keeping beat, urging them to come home.

The baby tiger held her paw up. Tess remembered the needle in her pocket. As Tess touched the needle, all of them were bathed in ribbons of lights. She pulled the needle out from her pocket and held it up against the glass, and it was as if rays of light cascaded down, red, blue, yellow, green, white, silver, gold, like the sun beaming light through a prism.

The footsteps were louder now, closer, but they kept screaming.

Julian pulled his violin from his shoulder case and began to play just one note, the bow artfully placed on one string as the purest sound, the highest note imaginable, rang through the air, the simple tone of it seeming to almost break the glass alone. Like shards of colored glass shattering around them.

And then it was ice-cold, as the glass turned a deep silver color like mercury, if mercury could shatter.

But curiously it was only the one pane that shattered, and it morphed, as it had before, into a kaleidoscope of images, turning to triangles of multicolored glass again, and a tiny hole appeared, almost the size of a pin or a needle.

Anna stepped up and did that same thing Alexei did. With her index finger poised and aimed, she darted her finger, unmindful of the shattered glass, right into the hole, forming a bigger hole as she pressed her finger farther through and then her hand, and the hole widened even more.

They helped Julian through first. Then Max. Then Tess. Then Anna stepped through, and they were back to where they'd started, in the original House of Mirrors. Almost home again, well, not really, but almost a sigh of relief. But then a barrage of footsteps were heard coming towards them. The footsteps got closer, and Lorenzo loomed threateningly, his face in multiples reflected in the glass, as if there was no way to escape Lorenzo head-on, threatening to push them back through the glass and into The Ghost Carnival.

"No one told you. No one told you you could come back here," he screamed threateningly, as he raised his hands to push them and they realized he was also holding a large cane as if he meant to snare them in its curve and push them back through the glass. One at a time if he had to.

A cry was heard. Like a roar in the jungle that reverberated against the glass. The baby tiger growled ferociously, jaws open, sharp nails straight out, poised to attack, and the baby tiger jumped and forcefully pushed Lorenzo with the strength of one paw, and threw Lorenzo through the glass into The Ghost Carnival, leaving behind a sparkling blast of color like a fireworks display on ice, splattered across the shattered glass pane.

Tess, Max, Anna, and Julian stood absolutely still and watched as the brightly colored strips of glass turned like a kaleidoscope again, reshaped, floral shapes you could get lost in, and reformed, into triangles that were only silver and realigned into a single pane of glass. And once again, The House of Mirrors was intact, as if the pane of glass had never shattered, at all. And the clock stopped ticking. And they were safe and back on the other side.

Tess looked down, but the baby tiger had curiously

disappeared. If the baby tiger had ever been there at all.

Lorenzo was gone. For a moment they saw a ghostly spectre of him, pale, his face frozen in a shock of anger, on the other side of the glass, where it looked like he belonged. The dark white clown standing beside him, smiling. And then the image faded. And the mirror seemed to close up, solidify, as if it was just a simple mirror now, and all they could see was their own reflections in the glass.

They heard a strange thud and then a grating noise as if The House of Mirrors had moved somehow and settled on the ground.

There was a couple standing next to Tess holding a baby, showing the baby its reflection in the glass, quite oblivious to the fact that anything peculiar had happened. Tess was already relieved to see that the baby's mother was eating a pink candyfloss.

Max started to confidently lead them out of The House of Mirrors. Max in front, then Julian and Anna, and Tess following behind. Max was leading them back to the entrance where they'd started.

They ran into another kid who was marveling at his own multiple reflections and eating a large lollipop as he admired himself. He shook his head at them. "You're going the wrong way," said the kid. Tess was quite relieved he had a British accent.

"That all depends on your point of view," said Tess, finding her attitude again. "We were lost, and we've always been taught it's a good idea to get back to where you started if you can."

back to where they started?

They were safe. They were back at the fair. Really back at the Fun Fair. The original one. Or at least it seemed that way. They could see the brontosaurus looming large in the distance. "Max, look," said Tess.

"I see it." He linked his pinkie to hers, not quite certain that they *were* safe. But he could smell the salt in the air, as if they were near a seashore. And the pine trees were gone. Or at least there were none in sight.

The concrete stools in the shape of mushrooms were there. And there was a sign on the food stand that said GRILLED SAUSAGES. It wasn't advertising MEAT PIES. That was very reassuring.

Still, they walked cautiously, not quite certain that they *were* safe. Anna led them now, ballerina-like, almost noiselessly, through the very crowded carnival to the back of the blue tent. Anna stopped and held her finger up.

"No. This one's mine," said Tess. Tess pulled the needle out from her pocket. She held it up, and it sparkled, as it always did in the sun, and with the sharp point executed her own version of what Alexei and Anna had done with their index fingers, a direct poke in with the sharp point of the needle, then straight down, splitting the tent and holding it open like a curtain. She let Anna through first and then Julian, then Max, then she followed in behind them. Anna smiled once they were inside, and with her own version of magic, using just her index finger, Anna zipped the tent up closed behind them.

There were screams of delight, pure joy, and happiness from Tatiana and Alexei, and a three-way hug that seemed as if it might never end. "Look at the two of you," said Anna, remarking how amazing Tatiana and Alexei looked. "I was so worried about you."

"We were a little worried about you, too," said Tatiana. And she hugged her sister again with a smile on her face and tears that were from joy.

"Thank you!" Tatiana said to Tess.

"Don't I get a thank you, too?" said Max, showing he had a little bit of attitude, too, and pride.

"Of course you do," said Tatiana, and she threw her arms around him, embarrassing him all the more.

Julian just stood there with his arms folded. He was staring at Tara, who was quietly standing behind Alexei and Tatiana. Tess saw them staring at each other with a look that was almost more powerful than any of the hugs and shrieks and screams of delight. It reminded her of what her mother called "unconditional love," a look she sometimes saw her parents exchange, the look in their dad's eyes as he smiled when he first saw her or Max after he'd been away or even sometimes just because they'd walked into the room, a look of pure love. It made Tess wonder what the connection was between Tara and Julian.

But then Tara looked at Tess and said, "I wasn't sure I was ever going to see you again."

"Really?" said Tess. "I thought you could see the future."

"Not always," said Tara, "but I knew that I was right to

take a chance on you." Her voice got softer. "I had a feeling from the moment I first saw you," said Tara, "that you could touch the sky."

"I couldn't have done it without Max," said Tess. "He's the one who always helped me find the way." Tess didn't mention the needle or the baby tiger.

the brontosaurus at one thirty

Aunt Evie was waiting for them at the Dinosaur Ride. The brontosaurus at one thirty, as they'd promised. It was obvious from the look on Aunt Evie's face and the fact that she was practically tapping her foot that they were a little late. *How late were they? They didn't know.*

"Where have you been?" said Aunt Evie. "You missed all the excitement. A baby tiger escaped from the zoo. And they had to send a zookeeper and a net. And people were screaming. And, well, it was very exciting."

Somehow that didn't surprise them.

Max looked at his iPhone, which was working again and had more than a three-quarters charge. It said: 1:35. "One thirty-five," said Max.

He and Tess exchanged a look and both shook their heads. *1:35?* But they both knew. They'd had an adventure like this before in England where time and place seem to have an equation of their own.

"I can't believe you missed the tiger," said Aunt Evie. "She was very adorable. The zookeeper said she was a she."

"We're not sure how she found her way in," said Tara, who'd come up behind them. "It almost seemed as if she was looking for something." This was said with a funny lilt in her voice as if she was almost teasing them.

"Aunt Evie, this is Tara. She takes care of, I think this is right, the kids who act in the aerial ballet show. We bought tickets for all three of us. Advance tickets. We thought it would be something you'd want to see. That's right, isn't it, Tara? You're the guardian for the Breathtaking Baranovas? That's what they're called, Aunt Evie. And apparently today they're performing, all three of them together for the first time in almost a year."

"Yes," said Tara. "That's one of the things I do, that and other things. Oh, my, it's almost two o'clock," she said. "You don't want to miss the show, do you? I hear it's going to be quite spectacular."

Tess and Max were certain she was right.

almost show time

The show was sold-out. The big blue tent was full to the bleachers. Apparently, they had "special" tickets in the first row. That was curious, Tess didn't remember buying "special" tickets, but their tickets had a star on them, and the usher led them down to the very center of the front row.

Tess looked around. She saw Julian in the back of the tent stand up from one of the last rows. He put on his backpack and slung his violin over his shoulder.

She whispered to Aunt Evie that she'd be right back.

She saw Julian slip out the blue silk curtain of the tent, literally slip out, he just lifted up the bottom and slipped right out.

Tess ran up the aisle. And then slipped out of the tent herself onto the carnival grounds. Tess didn't see him at first. But then she did. Up ahead. A solitary figure walking alone. His backpack hanging over his back, his violin hanging jauntily from his shoulder, his long straight hair as shiny as it had been the first day they'd met.

She'd almost caught up to him.

He was walking toward the entrance, or in this case the exit, to the carnival.

"Wait, Julian. Wait."

He turned and smiled at Tess.

"M'work's done here," he said. "For now, anyway. And it's time for me to carry on."

"But, but," she said, almost pleading, "are you sure they'll be okay without you?"

"Don't worry, Tess. It was just my job to take care of Anna until you brought her home. Until we brought her home. Tara'll find me if she needs me, and she'll stop by if she wants to. Tara has her ways. And sometimes, I promise," he said, putting his hand on Tess's cheek, "I promise this is true, sometimes one of you will look at something that brings back a memory, or hear a song that sounds familiar, and you'll know I never left you after all."

She started to say good-bye to him, throw her arms around his neck, but he shook his head and said, "Remember, sometimes the best way to see someone again is not to say good-bye."

He turned then. There wasn't any stopping him, his violin in its case slung over his shoulder, his backpack on his back, and walked out the carnival gates alone. And, sadly, Tess understood that it was time for him to "carry on."

the breathtaking baranovas touch the sky

The crowd was cheering. The show hadn't even started and the audience was already giving a standing ovation to an empty stage. And then a somewhat familiar face appeared. It was Ben the grill master. Except he wasn't a grill master any more. He was wearing a top hat and carrying a cane, his curly ringlets cascading around his smiling face. He seemed to be the new owner of the carnival, as the sign behind on the curtain read:

BEN'S FANTASTIC
FUN FAIR

Certainly Ben was the one in charge. He was holding a bullhorn, painted in circular swirls of red and white stripes, like a festive candy cane.

"Announcing," Ben said excitedly through the bullhorn, "reunited for the first time in a year . . . *Alexei, Tatiana, and Anna, The Breathtaking Baranovas* . . . performing again on the same stage!"

The curtain pulled back, and the aerial trapeze set was revealed with a dark blue sky painted on the ceiling dotted with silver stars that glowed and sparkled.

Alexei was already up on the platform. Tatiana was already across from him on another platform.

As Anna took the stage in a somewhat familiar costume, decorated with stars. She climbed the silver rope ladder, so quickly it was almost as if she was already flying. So delicate. So graceful. And at the same time so extraordinarily powerful that it was hard to keep your eyes off her.

Except that Alexei executed a triple somersault from the platform and grabbed on to a silver bar. He did that same thing again, pulling himself into a pretzel, sitting on the bar, and then flipping over so that he was hanging by his knees. Tatiana followed. Flew from a bar into a triple somersault and landed perfectly, grasping on to Alexei's hands as the two of them flew through the air, almost as if they were one. A drumbeat. And then the unmistakable sound of a violin, one note. Just for a moment, that pure clean sound, that Tess knew she would recognize always.

Anna took to the air, holding on to a silver bar, and vaulted through the air herself as if she was flying, bathed in a halo of light, and an orchestral soundtrack started slowly, violins, the shrill high note of a saxophone, punctuated by a deep bass drum.

As if from nowhere, a silver tightrope dropped from the ceiling—a tightrope that was an absolute circle, like a hula hoop or lasso, framing Tatiana and Alexei as they continued to swing through the air.

With a dancer's extraordinary poise and grace, Anna let go of the silver bar and landed on one toe on the edge of the tightrope, walking on pointe, her ballet shoes' heels never touching the silver cord as she performed a prima ballerina's dance, with an abundance of twirls and pirouettes around them on the thin edge of the tightrope, spinning so quickly that all of them seemed washed in a sparkle of silvery light.

"It's amazing what they can do with special effects and spotlights these days," said Aunt Evie.

Neither Tess or Max said a word, but they both knew it was simply Carnival Magic . . .

the sound of a violin

That was amazing," said Aunt Evie. "Really amazing. I don't think I've ever seen anything quite like it," she said. "They were so graceful, almost magical. To think someone could run on pointe like that on a tightrope. And they were so young."

Max was very quiet. Wistful almost. It occurred to him that he wasn't going to see the twins again, or Anna. There was something about this that made him sad, mournful, even though he was happy about the way everything had turned out. But Anna was so brave and fearless and extraordinary. His sister was fearless. But even on a good day, he couldn't imagine Tess wing walking. Well, maybe he could, but he wasn't going to try to imagine that.

Tess was quiet, too. She couldn't believe that she might never see Alexei and Tatiana and Anna again. Is that what England was going to be like, a place where you made friends who you were never going to see again? She stopped herself from thinking that. It truly had been a magical adventure. At least she thought it had. Maybe she'd imagined it, after all. Her head hurt. Maybe she'd really hurt her head when she'd rescued that kid from the Ferris wheel.

"Do you think we should go back and . . ."

Tess interrupted Max before he could even finish the sentence, the end of which was "go backstage and say good-bye."

"No," said Tess. "I definitely think we should not do that." She echoed Julian. "Sometimes the best way of making sure you might see someone again is by not saying, 'good-bye.' Besides, they did that thing with us when they were on the stage."

The Breathtaking Baranovas had still been doing curtain calls. The crowd was wild and this was the fourth time they'd come back on stage to take a bow. And all three of them looked directly at Tess and Max this time and put their hands up in the air, Anna in the middle, Alexei and Tatiana on either side, and linking pinkies executed a pinkie swear. Tess and Max, as if by instinct, did the same thing back. A pinkie swear meant forever. And in that extraordinary acknowledgement, there wasn't any reason to say a formal good-bye.

The gatekeeper had let them out, and as he did, he said, "Thank you again, M'Lady," to Tess. She looked at him and realized it was the same gatekeeper who had been at the zoo.

Aunt Evie hurried them to the car. The Bentley was parked in the first spot. "I tipped the ticket taker," said Aunt Evie, quite proud of herself. "Well, at least I tried to, but he wouldn't take five pounds from me, insisted he'd saved me the spot. Didn't make much sense really, since how could he have known that I was coming?"

But Tess, who'd met the ticket taker before, wasn't at all surprised he'd said this.

Aunt Evie had put the top down, even though the sun was setting. It was remarkable to look up at the clear sky, the proper shade of blue, exactly the way it was supposed to be, Aunt Evie and Max in the front seat, and everything comfortingly normal.

"I bought a roast chicken," said Aunt Evie. "Roast chicken's very good," she announced, "when it's almost room temperature. It's one of those foods you don't even have to heat up. And we have fresh rolls, a little bit of potato salad. I bought an interesting peach chutney that I thought we should try."

But Tess wasn't paying attention to her at the moment. She had looked over to the side of the road, and there was the traveller's wagon and a gentleman who looked a lot like Julian, sitting in a folding chair and playing the violin, and next to him, as if by magic, a horse that looked an awful lot like Coco. And sitting on the branch of a white birch tree, outlined against the dark brown edge of the peeling bark, a white dove, quietly flapping its wings almost as if it was dancing in a soft accompaniment to the violin. She remembered when Tara had seemed to morph into a dove when Alexei told them the bedtime story and now Tess was sure she hadn't imagined it.

Tess tapped Max on the shoulder. Max turned around and nodded, confirming he was seeing it, too, the white dove flapping its wings softly in the air almost as if it was dancing quietly to the music. Tess remembered what Julian had said to her when he was leaving, "Tara knows how to find me if she wants to." Tess looked carefully at the white dove so that she would always remember it.

The sound of the violin reverberated through the air, like a soft melody, a wistful tune and, in that moment, Tess knew that one day she might have the chance to hear it again.

traveller's wagon

carnival tent

airfield

olive grove

invisible wall

the house of mirrors

acknowledgements

I want to thank John Pearce, my high school science teacher, a master of physics, astronomy, and an understanding of the science of ecology almost before its time. I wish he was able to read this, but I am certain he knew that he deeply influenced the ways in which I see the world and—I can't be sure of this—but I also think he believed in magic; my own sisters, Nora, Delia, and Hallie and ditto the amazing and informative sibling relationships of my own children, step-children, nephews, and nieces, who, despite all our differences and occasional fights over a monopoly board, deeply know that we have each other's backs, pinkie swear; the extraordinary Jill Santopolo, whose remarkable acumen, attention to detail, no matter how much might be going on, elegant and exacting eye, and enthusiasm, are immeasurable, and I feel enormous gratitude for having her in my life; Michael Green, whose humor, warmth, and support mean more to me than he will ever know, not to mention his kindness for allowing me to publish under his umbrella; my husband, Alan Rader, whose unflagging belief in me and love I carry with me everywhere; also my friends Sally Singer, Holly Palance, Laraine Newman, Allison Thomas, Nick Pileggi, and John Byers for their love, kindness, generosity, and guidance; Kari Stuart, Amanda Urban, Bob Myman, Lindsay Boggs, and Talia Benamy, whose attention to detail, constant support, and sparks of brilliance have made these books a total delight to write and to publish; and to all the kids out there who sometimes believe in magic, believe in themselves, and vow to try to touch the sky!

Go to the next page to read a sample
of the next book in the adventures of
Tess and Max

THE
OTHER SIDE
OF THE
WALL

maybe it's the wind

"Did you see that?"

"See what?" Max replied.

"That . . . that shadow that went past the window,"
said Tess, "out in the garden." *It was more than a
shadow, a shape that had streaked by the window.* She
couldn't explain what it was.

Tess and Max were sharing a suite at a small, somewhat
trendy hotel in London called **The Sanborn House**.

They had gone to meet their mom and dad and Aunt Evie for Christmas break, although their parents hadn't arrived yet.

Tess would be sleeping in the bedroom. Max had a rollaway cot in the living room. At the moment, Tess was sitting on the antique carpet on the floor of the living room and Max was lying on his freshly made cot. They had checked in at the desk with Aunt Evie, found their hotel room, and obediently unpacked their suitcases.

They were both a little tired from the trip to London. Tess was staring vacantly out the window to the garden. Except she'd noticed something. Or at least she thought she had. It looked like a shape that had streaked quickly past the window—not an animal, something else, shadowy, which had sneaked past, not blown by the wind.

"I didn't see anything," said Max immediately, definitively, even though he was sitting up as if he had.

"But," he added, "there could be a number of explanations for it." There was a bit of an edge to his voice, as if he was irritated at Tess. And Tess noticed she hadn't told him, at all, what she'd seen and nonetheless he was rationalizing it for her. Ever logical, he explained, "For instance, a cloud passed across the sun, causing a shadow."

2

"We're in London, there isn't any sun," said Tess, not meaning to be funny.

Max hesitated, and then suggested gruffly, as if he wished this conversation would be over, "A large truck passed by in the alley then and altered the light."

"I don't think there is an alley," said Tess. "It looks like there's just a garden that separates our hotel from the back of the house on the street behind us. I bet the garden's pretty in the spring," she added.

"It's pretty now," said Max.

It was unusually cold, and the branches of the trees were gilded with ice and an occasional dangling icicle that oddly reflected what little light there was into colored patterns, the way a glass prism would.

"You're right," said Tess. "It is pretty. And the icicles are natural holiday tree decorations. I bet Mom would like them. And see those red berries dotting that bush? I wonder what kind of berry bush it is."

Max almost snapped at her, "Can we look it up before we test one? Or at least ask someone what it is?"

"Promise," said Tess who started laughing for a second until she realized Max hadn't meant *that* to be funny. She hesitated. "You didn't see anything? Really?!" she asked again. "But, what I saw was, umm"—she didn't really want to use the word, but she couldn't help it—"ghostly."

The wind was blowing, as if in punctuation, a cold and scary wind, rattling the windows.

"Okay, shadowy, then," said Tess modifying her thought so as not to frighten Max unnecessarily. "You didn't see it?" she repeated.

But before Max could answer, Aunt Evie burst in to their hotel room without knocking. "Oh my," she said, "put on your hat and grab your mittens."

She probably meant, put on your mittens and grab your hat, but neither one of them corrected her.

"I think it's going to snow," Aunt Evie said. "It never snows in London. Well, hardly ever. And when it does," she said, "it's a very magical time to go out."